THE ROCKING CHAIR

THE ROCKING CHAIR

FRANCES Y. McHUGH

G.K. Hall & Co.   •   **Chivers Press**
Thorndike, Maine USA   **Bath, England**

This Large Print edition is published by G.K. Hall & Co., USA
and by Chivers Press, England.

Published in 2001 in the U.S. by arrangement with
Maureen Moran Agency.

Published in 2001 in the U.K. by arrangement with the author.

U.S. Softcover   0-7838-9463-5 (Paperback Series Edition)
U.K. Hardcover 0-7540-4580-3 (Chivers Large Print)

The text of this Large Print edition is unabridged.
Other aspects of the book may vary from the original edition.

Set in 16 pt. Plantin by Minnie B. Raven.

Printed in the United States on permanent paper.

British Library Cataloguing-in-Publication Data available

Library of Congress Cataloging-in-Publication Data

McHugh, Frances Y.
    The rocking chair / by Frances Y. McHugh.
        p. cm.
    ISBN 0-7838-9463-5 (lg. print : sc : alk. paper)
    1. Actresses — Fiction.   2. New England — Fiction.
3. Haunted houses — Fiction.   4. Large type books.   I. Title.
PS3563.C3685 R64 2001
    813´.54—dc21   2001024177

THE ROCKING CHAIR

Chapter One

When Dirk Halburton called me and told me he had written a movie and that he and Tony Maretti were going to film it themselves, I asked, "How can you do that?"

He said, "Easy. Tony has an Arriflex camera and a tape recorder, and I have all the lights from my little theater, and I've recently inherited a big old-fashioned house up in Massachusetts. You remember me speaking of my Aunt Suzy?"

I said, "Yes."

"Well, she died and left me her house."

I said, "Oh, I'm sorry. That she died, I mean."

He said, "Yes, so am I. But about the house — it's an interesting old place. It dates back to the Revolution. One of those 'Washington Slept Here' type of places, complete with a get-away tunnel that comes out on the far side of a back field. I got the idea of doing a story in and around it to save money on locations. How about you being my leading lady? I'm going to direct the picture, and Tony is going to film it."

I laughed. "You're kidding, of course."

"No. I'm serious. Naturally, we've got to do the picture on the proverbial shoestring, as a show case, so I'll have to get friends to play all the parts. If it sells, we will all be riding the gravy train. Come on; be a sport."

Dirk knew I'd been doing a few TV commercials, but not enough to keep the wolf comfortably far enough away from my Carnegie Hall studio apartment for me to be able to relax. Occasionally I got a bit part in an off Broadway show. But nobody ever bought a diamond tiara on that.

When I didn't answer, Dirk said, "It's a very nice place. You'd like it. It's in a little Massachusetts village called Mount Sharon, and it's just up the road from the village green. You know the kind — white-steepled churches and a cannon on the green. It's New England according to Grandma Moses."

"Is Helen coming?"

He hesitated. "No. She has the kid, and with all the rest of us up there — well, you know Helen. She isn't in sympathy with my theater projects."

I couldn't answer that, because I did know how his wife Helen felt about his bent for the theater. A few years back he had started to show case theater down on West Broadway, worked like a dog fixing it up; then when it was catching on, he'd been closed because he didn't have some kind of license he'd never heard of. It just about broke his heart, but it would have been too expensive to fight the court order. And Helen was glad, because even with Dirk and his friends doing most of the work, they had sunk considerable money in the place.

"I was thinking," Dirk said, "if you would come up, you could help me. Be my hostess, sort of oversee things."

I gulped at that and was glad we didn't have visual color telephone, because I could feel my face getting red. You see, Dirk and I used to have a thing about each other, and almost got married one time. Then he met Helen, who is a cute blonde, and that was that. I'm not cute and I'm not even a Clairol blonde. I'm tall and — I guess the word is willowy. My hair is a dark auburn, and I leave it that way, in a longish feather cut. My eyes are the color of cream sherry and have chrome yellow flecks in them. Of course I darken my lashes and use a touch of green eye shadow, and that makes my eyes more noticeable than they otherwise would be. My teeth are good, thank heaven, but my mouth is larger than I would like to have it. No rosebud, I can assure you. And I am supposed to be a good sport, heaven help me. A reputation like that is poison, as far as romance is concerned.

Dirk knew I still carried a somewhat flickering torch for him and would do anything I could to help, and he was always one to follow up an advantage. So he kept on talking. "It's a natural, Cheryl," he persisted. "It can't miss. It's got everything. I've written the script especially around this house. It's sure to sell, and then we'll all be made. And it's just the break

9

you need. You can't go on taking antihistamine pills on TV forever. You're star material, and this is your big chance."

He knew he had me there. Naturally, every actress thinks she is star material and that all she needs is a break. And most of us grab anything that has potential, always in the hope that this will be it.

I could feel myself weakening as his persuasive voice came over the wire into my reluctant ear. He said, "Tony thinks we can do it in a couple of weeks. We'll all stay at the house, so it won't cost anybody anything, except for food. We can split the cost of that. After all, each of us has to eat anyway, so it won't be costing anybody any more, or as much, as if we stayed home. And we can take turns cooking and all that. The house is furnished, and my aunt put in modern conveniences like bathrooms, a dishwasher, clothes washer and dryer. And, believe it or not, she even had a telephone extension in one of the johns, because the house is so big she couldn't be running around answering phones that weren't near at hand. She was eighty-two when she died last year."

I drew in a defensive breath. "Who else have you asked?"

He said, "Well, I thought Vicki Chalmers would be good for the second lead. And I'll take a small part in the beginning. The rest of the time I'll be directing, and I can help Tony with the lights."

"Who else is coming?"

"John Lovell, for the lead opposite you."

I let out a yell at that. "Oh, Dirk!" I cried. "You *know* John and I don't get along!"

"So forget it for a couple of weeks. He's perfect for the part. And his name is getting to be known. He says he'll arrange to work it in, as a favor to me."

"That settles it then. I will not spend two weeks in the same house with John Lovell. He is conceited, he is disagreeable, he thinks he is God's gift to women, and he doesn't like me."

"Oh, for heaven sakes, come off it! He doesn't dislike anybody. He is really a good guy when you get to know him."

"Ha! I did get to know him — once."

"Well then —"

"He told me I was a lousy actress and always would be, so I might as well give up and get married."

Dirk laughed. "To whom? Him?"

"Well, he did have that in mind at the time. It was just after you and Helen were married and you'd had him over to dinner. The domestic set-up got to him, momentarily."

Dirk said, "Yeah. Helen is a good cook. And she had that first place of ours fixed up so it looked like something out of *House & Garden*."

"Well, I can cook too, but it's not my vocation. And the fact he was making more money than I was didn't make him a good actor."

"He's been doing all right in his TV series, *Stars Away.*"

"If you call that *good.*"

"It's got a high rating. And he's crying all the way to the bank with his pay checks."

"Well, anyway, I want none of him. So you can count me out. And good luck to you."

"Oh, Cheryl, don't be like that! I need you. I really do. You'd *make* the picture. You have such good style, and you're just the type for the part. And I'm getting Ada and Charlie Simmons for a couple of small parts. They haven't had anything lately, and they're willing to take a chance on this. Charlie's been sick, and a couple of weeks in the country will be good for him. And being as how they are a middle-aged married couple, they will be good chaperones, if anybody thinks we need chaperones."

"The natives probably will. What are the natives going to think of it all?"

"I hope they will be interested. Aren't the natives always interested when a movie is made in their town?"

"If they aren't, they sue you."

"I'm not worried. Just as long as my second cousin Harvey keeps out of my way."

"Who is he?"

"Oh, he's my grandfather's brother's son. He's about ten years older than I am, and whenever we met as kids we always got in a fight, and I always won even if I was smaller than he was."

"That should make for a friendly atmosphere at this point."

"You're so right. And not only that, but he always thought Aunt Suzy was going to leave him the house. Well, all he got were a few pieces of furniture and five thousand dollars."

"And all you got was the house?"

"And five thousand. But Helen doesn't want me to spend any of it. She says it should be put into the bank and left to grow for Billy's college."

"Was that all the money there was?"

"As far as I know. Aunt Suzy always lived comfortably. And as she got older, she didn't worry about spending her principal. I don't blame her. I think she was smart. Uncle Robert was as tight as the bark on a tree, so when he died, twenty years ago, she began to live it up, in a modest way, of course."

"Where does this Harvey live?"

"In Mount Sharon, I'm sorry to say. He is vice president of the bank, superintendent of the Sunday school in the Presbyterian church, active in the Lions Club, all that kind of thing. And his wife belongs to the Women's Club, a garden club, a bridge club, et cetera, et cetera."

"I understand. And again I say, good luck to you."

"Ah, come on, Cheryl. Don't turn me down. I promise to keep John Lovell in line. You won't have to see much of him. And there will be Vicki to amuse him."

"What you don't know, my dear Dirk, is that Vicki adores John and that John has told her several times to run along and play with her dolls and let him alone. So you've got trouble on your hands with that combination, as well as with John and me."

Dirk sighed. "You aren't helping any. Why can't you think of *me* a little? I've got a good thing going in this. I was hoping it would lift me out of that advertising agency that is giving me ulcers, and I was also thinking it would get you out of the rut of commercials. So why can't you cooperate? Or are you afraid of *me?*"

That did it! "That is a ridiculous thing to say!" I cried.

He chuckled. "Then come on. If Helen doesn't mind our being in the same house together for a couple of weeks, why should you? And there will be Charlie and Ada. It will all be perfectly proper."

I sighed. "Oh, all right. When do you start shooting?"

"The week after next. I'll call you and tell you the exact time later."

"All right," I finally gave in.

Chapter Two

To make a long story short, we were supposed to arrive at the house the 10th of July, which was a Wednesday. Dirk was taking everybody up in his Volkswagen station wagon, together with the lights and all the other paraphernalia. I was driving up in my old chevy. I preferred to do that so I would be free to get away by myself if things ever got too complicated, as far as human relations were concerned.

Dirk had told me it would take about four hours from the city, give or take a little, depending on how many times I stopped to eat on the way. Well, to be exact, it took me a little over four hours, even though I stopped once on the way, for some lunch at a Howard Johnson's.

It was after one when I came into the typical New England village of Mount Sharon, and when I saw it I was instantly enchanted. There was a pretty little village green at the cross-roads, with large old trees and well tended lawns. A few benches were placed along the edge; on them sat several elderly men and a woman watching a small child climb on an old cannon, which must surely have dated back to the Revolution. There was a drinking fountain and a decorative fountain.

On the periphery of the green were three churches, white-steepled as Dirk had promised. What I could see of the main street came to a dead end on the far side of the green. On the other side and across the road there were a few commercial establishments: a small lunchroom-type restaurant, a bakery, a tiny general store and a bowling alley.

I parked my car in front of the restaurant, got out and went in. There was a woman behind the counter near the cash register, and I asked her, "Can you tell me where the Manor House is?"

She was middle-aged, lean and shrewd-looking, and she eyed me suspiciously as she slammed shut the drawer of the cash register. "You aiming to buy it?" she asked.

I said, "No. I'm just visiting."

"There ain't no one up there," she told me.

With extreme pleasure I told her, "There will be, any minute now."

She rubbed her long sharp nose and carefully inspected me. "You got a key?" she asked.

I said, "No, but Mr. Halburton will be here, and he has a key. Mr. Dirk Halburton. He owns the place. But I suppose you know that."

"I knew some nephew got the place, but it was the wrong one."

I said, "Oh?"

She leaned a sharp elbow on the top of the cash register and put the other hand on her hip. "Yes," she said, all ready for a nice gossipy chat.

"Mr. Harvey, he's lived here all his life, and the place should have gone to him. But old lady Halburton, she up and left it to her other nephew who's one of them fly-by-night theater fellers."

I couldn't help smiling. "He works in an advertising agency," I told her, just to get her reaction.

"Same difference," she said, a gleam in her beady black eyes. *"Madison Avenue!"* She fairly spit the words at me across the cash register. "Madison Avenue — Broadway — they're all alike!"

I decided I'd had about enough of that, so I asked, "Would you be so kind as to tell me where the house is?"

She turned to the wide window, pointed to the right and said, "Up this road. At the top of the hill. You can't miss it. A big white house. Stands all by itself."

I said, "Thank you," and opened the screen door to go. But as I was stepping outside the woman said, "They say the place is haunted. You better be careful."

I turned and smiled at her. "Wonderful!" I said. "It sounds interesting."

Not waiting for her reply to that, I got in my car and drove slowly along the road. A few yards past the village green the road forked; one road going down a hill, the other going upward. I drove upward, and in a couple of minutes I saw the house, high on a green knoll above the road. It was beautiful: white clap-board, Georgian, spacious, inviting. A gravel driveway went up from the road, past the front of the house and over to a large sprawling barn. There was ample space to park and turn around. I drove over to the side so my car would be out of the way of Dirk's when he arrived. Then I got out and began to explore.

The front door of the house, at the top of four brick steps, had narrow windows on either side of it and a fan window above. I peeked in and could see through to a similar back door. The large center hall had a room opening from either side, the one to the right a living room with an enormous brick fireplace. The furniture was beautiful; priceless antiques and, on the wide board floors, oriental rugs of various sizes. A grandfather's clock stood in the hall. The room at the left of the center hall was a dining room, but I couldn't see into it very well.

I walked around the house. The flagstone walk was bordered with flowers, and near the back was a thick clustering of bushes. Out on the side of the hill which sloped down to the road were a couple of old apple trees, and there was a view of the village green; the white-steepled churches and across to rolling farm land. Somewhere in the near distance a rooster crowed. It was all very beautiful and peaceful, and in the bright sunshine of the July afternoon the idea of the house being haunted was too fantastic even to consider.

At the back of the house was a flagstone terrace in front of which was a swimming pool, now empty of water, and beyond, a large field of several acres of high grass, daisies and flowering weeds. At one side, beneath the kitchen window, was a rock garden, bright with rock pinks and whatever other small flowers they plant in rock gardens, and a peach tree at the end of the terrace. At the far side of the field was a small shack that appeared to be a tool storage place.

I decided to investigate the barn. The doors were latched but not locked. Pushing one open wide enough to slide in, I was intrigued by the size of the place. To begin with, it was beautifully built, with pegged beams of Gothic proportions and a row of twelve cow stalls right down the middle. Wandering around, I found abandoned chairs, broken sofas, and several mattresses slung over beams. One end, the one by the doors, had evidently been used as a garage, for there were oil spots on the floor, and an old tire and several outdated license plates were lying in a corner.

I went back outside and over to the front steps of the house. They were in the shade now and looked like a comfortable place for me to wait, and cooler than my car, which was in the sun.

I sat on the top step that made a small square porch and leaned back against the door, enjoying the view. I was going to like it here.

After a few minutes a large black cat walked regally around a lilac bush beside the barn, came over and looked at me. He had one white front paw and a white place on his neck and chest. His eyes were amber and looked very wise. I said, "Hello, pussy," and he came over and up the steps and, putting his front paws on my lap, said, "Meow."

I patted him and talked to him for a moment, and he jumped on my lap, turned around a couple of times and lay down with his front paws tucked under him. Then he began to purr. It was a soothing sound, and I closed my eyes. I guess we both went to sleep after that, because the next thing I knew a car was coming up the driveway and a horn honked. I jumped, frightening the cat, who leaped off my lap and ran in the direction of the barn door, which I had left partly open.

Yawning, I got to my feet and went to meet the people getting out of the car. Several voices called, "Hi!" and I answered, "Hi." It *would* be my luck to have John Lovell the first person to get out of the car and meet me face to face.

He was as handsome as ever, and the sight of him stirred my pulses in spite of my resolutions. He was six feet tall, broad-shouldered, with deep blue eyes and soft blond hair that he had let grow longer than I liked to see it. I don't go for the hippie style of long hair for men. However, I knew John had had to let his hair grow for his part in *Stars Away*. He had on tight dungarees and a red plaid sport shirt open at the neck. The sleeves of the shirt were folded up above his elbows and showed his powerful, golden-haired forearms. I said, "Hello, John," and he said, "Hi, Cheryl." He turned to Dirk, who had just gotten out of the driver's seat, and asked, "Where do you want us to put the lights and things?"

Dirk said, "Leave everything in the car until I open up the house." Then he grinned at me. "Hi, Cheryl," he said. "You must have made good time."

I said, "I started early," and decided Dirk still had that certain something: a *savoir faire*, casual good looks, with close-cropped brown hair parted on the side and brushed straight across, dark brown eyes, a lean, sinewy body and a ready smile. He looked equally well on Madison Avenue, on a stage, or in a living room. He patted me on the shoulder and said, "I guess you know everybody."

I said, "Yes," and made a point of ignoring John, as I greeted the rest of the company. I knew the Simmons' only casually, but in this kind of a situation, everybody was always familiar with everybody else. I was glad of the confusion that followed as everyone got out of the car and Dirk unlocked the front door of the house. We all trooped in behind him, and I asked, "Have you ever been here before?"

He said, "Oh yes. I used to visit Aunt Suzy

when I was a kid. And I went to Amherst, which isn't too far from here, so I used to come over once in a while. But this is the first time I've been here since last summer, when Aunt Suzy was taken sick."

We all stood in the hall looking around; then we began to wander in different directions. A wide staircase went up at the left. Also at the left was the entrance to the dining room, which was furnished with old-fashioned mahogany: a round table with a center pedestal and claw feet, a sideboard, a high chest of drawers, a tea wagon and six chairs — two armchairs and four straight-backed. The seats of the chairs were hand-made petitpoint.

A door at the back of this room opened into a large old-fashioned kitchen that had been modernized. From the kitchen there was a door to the outside at the end toward the barn, and opposite this door was one into the back of the center hall that came out near the back door to the terrace. The room was so large there was ample wall space for these doors, in addition to the kitchen equipment. Opening still another door, I found a flight of back stairs going up to the second floor, and there was another door into a walk-in pantry. Just beside the exit from the kitchen into the back part of the hall was another door that disclosed a powder room.

I could see that Tony was looking to see where he could set up his lights. He came over and put a casual arm around me as we left the kitchen and returned to the front of the center hall. "What do you think about it?" he asked me.

"Very charming," I said. "Don't you think?"

"Sure. Nice little pad," he said with a grin, and gave me a brotherly hug. I knew Tony casually but not intimately. We'd worked together a couple of times in off-Broadway things and palled around in groups, and I'd always found him to be pleasant, cooperative and completely impersonal. And he was an excellent actor. As far as I knew, he had never had a girl. He traveled with groups, was nice to every girl with whom he came into contact but never went out of his way to make an impression on any one girl.

He was five foot ten, with broad shoulders and a torso that tapered to a slender waist, and he looked marvelous in everything he wore, from swimming trunks to evening clothes. He had straight black hair, just touching his collar in back, with moderate sideburns and a forelock that often fell over his high forehead. His eyes were that liquid, velvety dark brown with long curved lashes that so many Italian men have. His skin, naturally olive, was always darkened either by the sun or a sun lamp. And his slow friendly smile showed a set of even white teeth. I would have liked to have had him for a brother. And I guess that about sums up Tony Maretti, as far as I knew him at that time.

The others had moved on into the living

room, and we followed. This room extended the entire depth of the house, with windows facing both front and back and a large window on either side of the fireplace, which was on the outside wall. The furnishings were grouped to divide the room into two sections, breaking the too long length. The front part had a really antique ebony square piano, and chairs and a sofa were placed in a conversation group. The back part of the room had a large sofa on either side of the fireplace with a low marble-topped table between. The back walls were lined with bookshelves crowded with all kinds of books. Aunt Suzy apparently had kept up with the times as far as her reading was concerned. Scattered about in the rest of the room were small tables and chairs and a few standing floor lamps. What wall space there was had a scenic paper, faded to pleasing aqua tints.

Looking around, Dirk said, "Nice, isn't it?"

We all agreed, and his eyes filled with tears. "Aunt Suzy knew how to live, bless her," he said.

"You were fond of her?" I asked him.

He nodded. "Very. It won't be the same with her gone. I used to like to visit here."

"But now you own the place," I reminded him.

"It won't be the same. Aunt Suzy won't be here."

Mrs. Simmons had wandered over to the piano and was playing softly. It was a Debussy *Arabesque*. I went over and stood beside the piano, and she looked up. "Don't stop," I said. So she went on playing softly.

Ada Simmons was a pretty fading blonde who had kept her hair touched up and always coiffed in whatever was the current style, but she had been unable to do anything about her thickening figure. However, when she had a part that called for a younger, thinner woman, she always seemed to get herself into a tight enough girdle to give the required effect.

Charlie, her husband of eighteen years, had been a comedy character actor and could still do his stuff whenever he got the chance. But for quite a while now he hadn't had anything. He was of medium height, a trifle heavier than he used to be, and his thinning hair and scraggly mustache, originally a light reddish brown — I guess you would call it sandy — now had considerable gray mixed in. It was rumored he had been drinking heavily lately, but today he seemed perfectly sober.

Ada stopped playing and looked around the room. I asked, "How do you like it?"

She shrugged. "There certainly seems to be space enough, and it is really lovely, but I'd die if I had to live way up here in the country. I like to hear a subway once in a while."

I smiled. "I don't believe I'd like it for too long a time," I admitted.

John had managed to keep as far away from me as possible since we'd come into the house, but he hadn't been that lucky with Vicki. Out of the corner of my eye I could see her sticking close to him and chatting with much animation, looking eagerly up into his face and giggling coquettishly.

Vicki was a cute girl; small, with a neat, if not voluptuous figure. She had good legs for miniskirts and her eyes were large and brown, but not the velvety brown of Tony's. I knew her hair was also brown, but she kept it platinum and wore it long and straight with bangs. And I had to admit that on her it looked good.

Ada left the piano, and suddenly Dirk was beside me. I asked, "What's this I hear about the house being haunted?"

"Where did you hear that?" He seemed surprised. "Sounds like something my dear cousin Harvey would circulate."

"The woman in the restaurant down by the village green told me. I stopped there to ask my way."

His lips tightened. "Oh, Annie Bradley, that old harridan," he snapped. "She's just angry because Harvey didn't get the house. She's a friend of his wife."

"Then there's no truth in it?"

The tightness left his lips, and he smiled. "Of course not. I'm surprised at you, Cheryl, a sensible, sophisticated city girl like you."

I answered his smile. "I'm almost disappointed. A ghost might be fun."

"I wouldn't mind if it was Aunt Suzy," Dirk said.

From across the room Vicki asked, "Can we go upstairs?"

Dirk said, "Sure. Come on." And we all followed him into the hall and up to the second floor.

This floor also had a center hall from which bedrooms and a couple of bathrooms opened. The biggest bedroom, connected with the biggest bathroom, the one with the extension phone on the wall beside the john, had unquestionably been Aunt Suzy's. There was a big canopy bed, a fireplace set in pine-paneled walls, built-in bookcases on either side of the fireplace, a Queen Anne highboy, a dressing table and several easy chairs and small tables. Beside each chair was a good reading light. On the wide board, highly polished floor were scattered hooked rugs.

In a corner beside a window was an old-fashioned rocking chair, and beside it a small round table on which was a large basket with some unfinished knitting in it. There were also a couple of hanks of wool and a pair of knitting needles.

Dirk said, "This was Aunt Suzy's room. I think I'll stake it off for Helen and me. The rest of you can take your pick of the other rooms." I noticed no one mentioned the fact that Helen wasn't there. So of course I didn't.

There was another large comfortable room across the hall with a four-poster bed. Dirk suggested, "Ada and Charlie can take this."

A somewhat smaller room at the front of the hall had twin beds. Dirk said, "How about this for Cheryl and Vicki?"

Vicki and I exchanged glances which were totally lacking in enthusiasm.

That left Tony and John. At the back of the hall, with windows overlooking the swimming pool and the back field, were two single rooms. Between them was a small bathroom. Dirk said, "I guess Tony and John get these."

"Fine," Tony said, and John said, "Perfect."

And so the station wagon was unloaded and the various bags put into the rooms where they belonged. Tony's Arriflex camera, the klieg lights, the tape recorder and a pile of 16-millimeter films were put into a corner of the dining room.

Chapter Three

Our dinner that first night was simple but adequate. There were hamburgers, frozen French fries, salad, ice cream and coffee.

Mrs. Simmons took over the preparation of the meal and to everybody's surprise was very efficient.

Dirk set the table, at the same time showing us girls where everything was, such as knives, forks, dishes, table linen, etc. To save on laundry, we decided on straw place mats instead of a tablecloth. And there were paper napkins which Dirk had brought.

When we finished dinner, I said, "Vicki and I will clean up."

Vicki tossed her head. "Speak for yourself," she said. "I want to take a walk. And I'd like to see what's inside that big barn."

Dirk said, "There's nothing out there to interest you. You stay here and help Cheryl. Tony and I want to go over the script so we can start shooting tomorrow. We've got to get this job done in two weeks. That's all the vacation I've got."

John said, "Yeah. I've got to get back, too. We are going to start rehearsals on next fall's *Stars Away* the end of July. They are using reruns for the summer."

Vicki pouted prettily, but it didn't get her anywhere. I said to Ada, "You go on now. You've done your share for today." She gave me a grateful smile and turned to Charlie. "Why don't you go out on the terrace and relax? I'll go upstairs and do our unpacking."

For answer Charlie just grunted, but he did get up from the table and go out on the terrace, where Dirk had put some wicker chairs and beach chairs.

Dirk said, "Come on, Tony. Come up to my room. We can work for a while up there."

John got up, saying, "I'll be out back with Charlie, if anybody wants me."

Vicki and I carried the soiled dishes out to the kitchen; then she went and stood looking out the screen door facing the barn, while I rinsed and stacked the dishes in the dishwasher. Suddenly she asked, "Why did you and John Lovell break up?"

Her question was such a surprise to me that I dropped a coffee cup, and the handle broke off. "Why should that matter to you?" I asked, trying to keep my temper under control.

"Because I am going to marry him myself, and I was just wondering." She turned from the door and sauntered over to where I was standing beside the sink. I turned on the dishwasher, and the water began to swish around efficiently, if somewhat noisily. I asked, "Has he asked you to marry him?"

She shook her head, and her long platinum hair shimmered. "Not yet," she said, "but he will, before we go back to the city."

Turning to clean the sink, I said, "I wouldn't count on it, if I were you."

"Why not?"

"Because I don't think John wants to get married."

"Just because he wouldn't marry you?"

I whirled around and faced her. I was angry now, and my hands were beginning to tremble. "Our engagement, or rather understanding, was broken off by mutual agreement. And if you're smart, you'll let John Lovell alone."

Her large brown eyes met mine challengingly. "So you can have another chance at him?"

I clenched my wet hands at my sides. "Stop it, Vicki! He'll hear you. Just mind your own business and let me and John alone."

She grinned at me impishly. "I'll let *you* alone all right, but I won't let John alone. And do you know why?"

"I'm not the least bit interested," I told her. I was breathless with anger and terrified for fear our voices were carrying out to the terrace, where I could see Charlie and John sitting smoking and chatting.

"Well, I'll tell you anyway," Vicki said. "Because *he* isn't going to let *me* alone, that's why. *You* just haven't got what it takes. You lost Dirk Halburton, and then you lost John Lovell. So what are you going to do now? Go after Tony?"

Of its own volition my wet right hand came up and slapped her cheek. She gasped and backed away from me, and it was at that moment a strange man knocked on the wood frame of the screen door. He must have walked up the driveway, because I hadn't heard a car. I knew he couldn't have helped but see me slap Vicki. But if he had, he didn't let on. He called, "Anybody home?" and peered through the screen.

I said, "Yes?"

He opened the screen door and stepped into the kitchen. "Dirk around?" he asked. He was about forty, tall, big in every way, with a red face and graying brown hair. His eyes were a light blue with a sharpness in them that made me feel cold. I said, "He's busy. Can I help you?"

He smiled and showed yellowish, uneven teeth. "I'm his cousin Harvey," he said. "I'd like to see him."

Before I could answer, Vicki said, "He's upstairs. I'll call him." She turned to go into the hall, but the man pushed past her. "I'll get him," he said. "I know my way around here." He had on gray slacks and a gray plaid sports jacket over a white shirt. He even had on a tie. As he went past me, I saw the back of him and noticed he had the beginning of a small bald spot on the top of his head.

I whirled on Vicki. "Why did you do that?" I demanded. "Dirk can't stand his cousin."

Vicki shrugged.

"I'm sure Dirk doesn't want to see him."

"Oh, for heaven sakes!" she snapped. "You make me sick!" She stalked out.

I finished in the kitchen, put out the lights and wandered into the living room to see if I could find a book. In a few minutes Dirk and Harvey came downstairs and into the living room. Dirk was saying, "I'm afraid I can't do that, Harvey." Then they saw me. Thinking they might want the room to themselves, I said, "I was just going up to my room. I've found a book to read."

But Dirk said, "No, don't go. I'd like you to meet my cousin, Harvey Halburton. Harvey, Miss Cheryl Daniels."

I said, "We've met."

I thought Harvey looked angry about something, but Dirk had a smile on his face. To the introduction Harvey said, "Yes, I've met the young lady." Then he asked, "What happened to the other one?"

I said, "Vicki? She's out on the back terrace."

Harvey said, "Let's go out there," and turned and left the room, heading for the back door and the terrace. As he passed me to follow his cousin, Dirk whispered, "Come on; I may need you." So with the book I'd chosen under my arm, I followed the two men out to the terrace.

Dirk introduced his cousin to John and Charlie. They both said a polite, "How do you do," and John stood up and shook hands with Harvey. Then, before John could sit down again, Vicki said, "Come sit by me, Harvey," and pulled the chair so John couldn't sit in it.

Dirk raised an eyebrow and gave me a quizzical look. Harvey quickly accepted Vicki's invitation and sat down beside her, which left John standing up with Dirk and me.

Dirk said, "I have to get back to Tony. He'll wonder where I am." He started to go into the house, but Harvey said, "What shall I tell Emma?"

Dirk shrugged. "Why not tell her what I told you?"

"She's not going to like it."

Dirk smiled wryly. "To put it bluntly, that's tough."

Harvey's already red face became redder. "You're making a mistake, Dirk."

"In what way?"

"In turning down a good offer."

Dirk's smile disappeared. "If that's the way you want to look at it, that's all right with me. If Aunt Suzy had wanted things different, she would have arranged for them to be."

"You're a fool, Dirk. You always were."

Vicki reached out a hand and patted Harvey's arm. "Come now, boys; don't fight."

For answer Dirk went into the house. John was sauntering across the terrace toward the barn, and I said, "Pardon me," and followed Dirk into the house. He was in the kitchen getting a couple of bottles of beer to take upstairs. When he saw me he asked, "Is Vicki giving you any trouble?"

I stood in the doorway, hugging my book. "Not really. Why?"

"I was just wondering. John isn't too happy about her being up here, and Tony doesn't seem to like her very much. *That* I didn't know."

I didn't make any comment, so he asked, "No phone calls?"

"No. Haven't you a phone in your room?"

"Yes. Two, as a matter of fact; one by the bed and one in the john."

"Well then, if the phone had rung you'd have heard it."

He took a bottle opener from a drawer, then two Pilsener-type glasses from a wall cupboard. With his back to me, he said, "That's right; I would have."

"You expecting a call?"

He swung around. "I thought maybe Helen would call."

"Why don't you call her?"

He looked carefully at the glasses, both of which he had in his left hand. "No," he said. He came toward the door, and I stepped aside so he could pass me. But when he reached me he stopped and looked down at me thoughtfully. "Sometimes I think I should have married you, Cheryl."

I took a step backward, away from him. "Oh no!" I cried. "Don't say that! Don't even think it!" Then, without saying good night, I hurried through the large center hall and ran up the stairs to my room.

I tried to read for a while but I couldn't keep my mind on the story, even though it was a very interesting foreign intrigue tale. After a while I decided I'd go to bed.

I must have dropped off to sleep for a while. Then something woke me. I listened and thought I heard someone crying. It seemed to be coming from the other side of the wall, where I knew Ada and Charlie were. Was Ada crying? And if so, why? But it soon stopped.

I glanced over at Vicki's bed and saw it was empty. I looked at a bedside clock that was on the night table between the two beds. It had a radium dial, and the hands were pointing to eleven-twenty. I wondered where Vicki was.

I went to sleep again but was awakened by something thumping against the door to the hall. I sat up in bed, listening. It sounded as if something were being thrown at it. My heartbeat quickened. What could it be? Or who? Had the woman in the restaurant been right? Was the house haunted? But how ridiculous!

The hands of the clock were now pointing to three, and Vicki's bed was still empty. I snapped on the reading light that was on the wall over the bed. Each bed had one. Then I got up, put on my robe and slippers and tiptoed to the door. I had to know what was being thumped against it. I opened the door quickly, so if anyone was there I would surprise him.

But the thing that was there was such a surprise to me I didn't know whether to laugh or cry.

Two large luminous eyes looked up at me, and the big black cat who had made friends with me in the afternoon said, "Meow," picked up a dead bird that was at his feet and put it down at mine.

I said, "Oh, no, thank you," and edged the bird out into the hall away from the door with my foot. I'd deal with it in the morning. Knowing cats and understanding them, I realized the bird was a present for me. When I rejected his present, the cat walked into the room with his long black silky tail waving in the air like a banner.

I leaned down and smoothed his back, and he rubbed against my ankles and followed me to my bed. Then he jumped up on the bed, sat down and looked at me accusingly.

"I didn't know you were in the house," I told him.

He blinked at me, closing and opening his eyes slowly.

"Who let you in?" I asked.

The cat blinked at me again, slowly.

I went back to the door, opened it again and stepped out into the hall to see if anyone was around. There wasn't a sound. The hall was dark and all the other doors were closed.

I returned to my room, closed the door, snapped off the light and got back into bed. It was then quarter past three.

Again I wondered where Vicki was.

Well, I wasn't going to worry about it now. So again I went to sleep, and the next thing I knew it was daylight, the sun was shining in the windows, and the bedside clock pointed to seven-thirty. Vicki's bed was still empty and hadn't been slept in all night.

Chapter Four

I was the first one downstairs, so I was the one who found Vicki asleep on one of the living room sofas.

I decided to let her alone and go out to the kitchen to start breakfast. In a few minutes she came out, yawning and rubbing her eyes. I was fixing frozen orange juice in a large glass pitcher. Vicki said, "Oh, am I tired!"

"Why didn't you come to bed last night?" I asked, stirring the liquid in the pitcher with a long-handled spoon.

She strolled across the kitchen, opened the side door and stood looking out toward the barn. A delightful smell of country came into the kitchen. I caught a breath of it and breathed deeply. Vicki said, "It was so late, or rather early, when we got home, I decided I'd better not disturb you."

"Where were you?"

"Taking a ride."

"With whom?"

"Harvey. Not that it's any of your business."

I tossed the long-handled spoon into the sink. "Harvey?" I almost screamed. "But he's married!"

She turned to me and smiled. "So?"

39

"And he's also Dirk's cousin."

"I know that."

"But why on earth would you go riding with Harvey?"

"Because I wanted to teach John Lovell a lesson."

I had to choke back the hysterical laugh that almost rushed out of me. "You've got to be kidding!"

She strolled over to me. "May I have some of that?" She nodded to the pitcher of orange juice.

I gave her a glass and said, "Help yourself."

She poured out a glass of juice and began drinking it. After the first few swallows she said, "No, I'm not kidding. John seems to think he's the only man who can attract girls. So I thought I'd show him he wasn't."

"But *Harvey!* Surely he's no competition for John Lovell."

"Sad but true. And the funny part of it is, Harvey thinks he is as irresistible as John."

I began getting the table silver out of a drawer, took the straw place mats from another drawer and went into the dining room. As I was setting the table, Dirk came down the stairs and, seeing me, came in. "Good morning," he said. "Did you sleep well?" He had an armful of scripts.

"Most of the time."

"Oh? Wasn't your bed comfortable?"

"Very."

"Something disturb you?"

I placed the last piece of flat silver on the table. "Well, for one thing, I had a visitor in the middle of the night."

"A visitor? Who?" Dirk's eyes began to flash.

I smiled. "Don't get excited. He had four feet."

For a moment he looked baffled; then he grinned. "Oh, Tommy?"

"Is that his name?"

"Yes. He was Aunt Suzy's cat. He always slept with her. I guess he's been staying with one of the neighbors."

"Then why didn't he go to your room?"

"He did, but I wouldn't let him in."

"He brought me a dead bird. It's on the floor in the hall near my door."

Dirk smiled. "I'll take care of it later. That's his way of showing you he likes you."

"How did you know he wanted to get into your room?"

"He has a trick of jumping at a closed door. It makes quite a noise."

I had to smile. "Yes, it does. I almost thought the family ghost was after me."

Dirk sobered instantly. "Speaking of ghosts," he said, "I think Aunt Suzy came to visit me last night."

I stared at him. "Dirk! You can't be serious!"

He ran a hand through his hair. "I don't know," he said thoughtfully. "I could have imagined her presence. I was thinking of her.

But thoughts won't make a rocking chair rock."

"Perhaps the wind?"

"There wasn't any in the part of the room where the rocking chair is, and the window beside it was closed. It was after Tony left me and went to his room. I undressed, took a shower, and when I returned to the bedroom the chair was rocking."

"Were the lights on?"

"Only the light on the table beside the bed. The others I'd turned off before I went into the bathroom."

"What did you do? About the chair, I mean."

"Foolishly I stood looking at it, and then I said, 'Is that you, Aunt Suzy?' "

"Then what happened?"

"The chair began to rock faster. Then it slowed down and stopped, and I — well, this sounds silly, but I felt something soft touch my cheek."

"As if someone had kissed you?"

He drew in a deep breath and looked at me almost as if he were ashamed. "Yes," he said.

"Were you frightened?"

He smiled then. "Of Aunt Suzy? Of course not."

I didn't know what to say and was glad that Ada and Charlie came down the stairs just then. They both said, "Good morning," and Dirk and I replied. I thought Ada's eyes looked red, as if she'd been crying, but Charlie appeared rested and cheerful.

Dirk said, "What does everybody want for breakfast?"

"I've already mixed the orange juice," I said. "Why don't we go out to the kitchen? Vicki is out there."

"No, she isn't," Ada said. "She came upstairs a couple of minutes ago."

I said, "Oh, I didn't notice."

"She came up the back stairs."

In the kitchen, Dirk said, "I want to get the pool filled right away. We'll have some shots in and around that."

"Doesn't it have to be cleaned out and scrubbed first?" I asked. Not that I knew anything about it, but I'd heard people talking.

Dirk said, "Yes. I should have had it attended to before we got here. I'll call Aunt Suzy's handyman and gardener, Joe Hinkley. He lives just down the road, and he'll take care of it. He can do it in a day. But in the meantime we can go ahead with some of the indoor shots. I have the scripts here." He started sorting them. "Here's yours, Ada." He gave her a black-bound script. "And yours, Charlie. And yours, Cheryl. I'll leave the rest of them here on the sideboard. As soon as everyone has had breakfast, we can sit out on the terrace and have a run-through. When the sun gets too hot, we can go into the living room. That's always nice and cool in the afternoon." He went to a wall phone to call the handyman, and I said, "I'll get breakfast if somebody will call John and

Tony. We can't eat in relays or we'll never get through."

"I'll go and wake them up," Dirk said, "as soon as I finish this call."

Ada and I went out to the kitchen, and Charlie sauntered onto the terrace. As I began getting out eggs, bacon, butter and bread for toast, Ada began filling glasses with orange juice.

I couldn't help asking, "Were you sick last night?"

She looked surprised. "No. Why?"

"I thought I heard you crying."

She put down the pitcher but held an empty glass in her left hand. "That wasn't me. I heard it too. I wondered if it was you or Vicki."

I didn't want to let her know Vicki hadn't come to bed all night, so I just said, "No, it wasn't either of us. But a cat woke me up, a big black cat. He used to belong to Dirk's aunt."

"Oh dear! I don't much like cats. I hope he stays away from me. Was it the one in your lap when we arrived yesterday?"

"Yes. He's perfectly harmless. In fact, he's very friendly."

Ada recommenced filling the glasses with orange juice. She said, "I didn't sleep too well, and I was standing at one of the windows just as it was beginning to get light, and I saw Vicki come in. She'd been out with some man in a car. He let her out down the road, and she walked up the driveway to the house."

44

I sighed. "Oh dear! Maybe one of us should talk to her. But I don't think she'd listen to me."

"Well, I scarcely know her." Ada put the filled glasses on a tray and took them into the dining room. Returning with the empty tray, she said, "I think Dirk is the one to speak to her. It's his house and his project."

"I guess you're right."

Tommy came walking into the kitchen, his tail waving in the air, and said, "Meow."

I said, "Good morning, Tommy." Then to Ada, "This is Tommy. He and I are very good friends."

Tommy rubbed against my ankles and arched his back, purring loudly.

Ada sidestepped. "Don't let him do that to me," she said. "Cats give me the creeps."

Having always liked cats, I never could understand anyone who didn't. "I'll give him a saucer of milk outside," I said. "That will get him out of the house."

The cat seemed hungry and was very willing to follow me out to the terrace, where I put the saucer of milk in a corner out of the way.

Charlie was sitting in one of the wicker chairs, reading his script. He looked up and said, "Hi, kittie," and the cat said, "Meow," but he wanted the milk more than a new friend.

I stood looking across the fields. It was a lovely morning. The grass was glistening with dew, and everything smelled sweet and fresh.

From above a man asked, "Do you always get up this early?"

I looked up. Tony was at the window of his room, buttoning his shirt.

I said, "Oh, good morning. Hurry up. I'm about to get breakfast. Is John up?"

"If he isn't, it isn't Dirk's fault. I think he's in the shower."

"Okay. Both of you hurry up."

"Be right down," Tony promised, and disappeared from the window.

I turned to Charlie. "Do you want eggs and bacon?" I asked.

"If it isn't too much trouble."

"How do you like your eggs?"

"Any way. Whatever the rest want."

Well, I thought, at least Charlie was agreeable.

Vicki didn't come down for breakfast, and when I went up after her she was sound asleep on her bed. I shook her gently. "Vicki, wake up. Breakfast."

She opened one eye and said, "Ugh! Go away."

I shook her again. "Come on, Vicki. Dirk wants to have a run-through of the script as soon as we finish breakfast."

She closed her eye. "Can't," she murmured.

"But you've got to! That's why we're here."

She said, "Um. Show must go on. Go away."

I could see there was no use trying to get her

up, so I left the room and closed the door. When I got downstairs, Dirk asked, "Is she coming?"

Everybody was sitting at the dining table, seemingly enjoying his breakfast. I sat down at my place. My egg was beginning to congeal. I said, "No. She's sleeping."

"Sleeping?" Dirk asked. "Didn't she sleep last night?"

I said, "I guess not much."

Dirk ran his hand through his hair. "But she can't sleep *now!*" he said crossly. "We've got to get going!"

I didn't say anything. I didn't want to cause any trouble. But Ada spoke for me. "You'll have to have a talk with Vicki, Dirk."

"About what?" Dirk gulped some coffee.

"About keeping late hours."

"What do you mean? We all went to bed fairly early last night."

"All but Vicki," Ada said.

Charlie said, "Keep still, Ada. Don't tattle."

"Tattle about what?" Dirk demanded. "What's all this about?"

Ada nibbled at a piece of toast. "Why don't you ask Vicki?" she said.

Dirk looked across the table at me. "Do you know anything about this?" he asked me.

I met his eyes and tried to keep mine blank. "Not much."

Dirk crumpled his paper napkin into a tight ball and threw it down onto his plate. "Damn it

47

all!" he cried. "If we're not all going to co-operate, we'll never get this picture in the can by the end of two weeks!"

Everyone had finished his breakfast, and John and Tony were lighting cigarettes. After the first puff of his, John asked, "Couldn't Helen play Vicki's part?"

Dirk's lips tightened. "Helen isn't here," he said. "Besides, she's not an actress."

"But Vicki's part isn't too difficult," Tony said, dipping the tip of his match in his empty coffee cup.

Dirk frowned. "If you didn't want to work with Vicki, why didn't you tell me before we got up here?"

Tony shrugged. "I thought maybe she'd grown up a little."

"Meaning?" Dirk lit a cigarette, shaking out the match and tossing it onto his egg-smeared plate. I shuddered. Those matches would have to be cleaned off the dishes before the dishes were put into the dishwasher.

Tony watched the smoke curling up from his cigarette. "Vicki likes to play around, have fun. She's a good kid, but she gets her values mixed sometimes."

The sound of a car coming up the driveway and stopping at the front door made us all glance at the front windows. Dirk got up and looked out, then said, "Oh! My God!"

I asked, "Who is it?"

He turned away from the window and went

to open the front door. "Emma," he said disgustedly.

Everybody looked questioningly at me. "I think she's Harvey's wife," I told them.

Ada craned her neck so she could see the car better. "It looks like the car Vicki came home in this morning," she said.

Charlie said, "Shut up!" and shook his head at her.

The woman who came in the front door was about five feet seven and thin, with practically no figure. Her hair was a dark red, the kind of a dye job that looks purple in the sun, and it was coiffed in a beehive style, undoubtedly done by a hairdresser who wasn't too expert. Her eyes were a dull brown, her features regular but sharp. She had on a sleeveless green linen shift that accentuated her lack of figure and her thin arms. The dress covered her knees, which was probably just as well. Under her right arm she had a large white straw purse, and on her left arm were at least half a dozen bracelets that jangled, one of which was a charm bracelet. She said, "Good morning, Dirk," and kissed his cheek.

Dirk took a step backward and closed the door.

I'm glad I found you home," she said. "Harvey told me you flatly refused our generous offer."

Dirk said, "That's right."

She smiled at him as if he were a naughty little boy and patted his arm. "Perhaps we can persuade you to change your mind."

Dirk said, "I think not."

The woman walked past Dirk and came to the dining room door. "Are these your friends?" she asked, looking us over carefully with one plucked eyebrow raised. I guessed her to be about thirty-seven or eight.

Dirk said, "Yes, these are my friends," and began to introduce us. "Mrs. Halburton — Cheryl Daniels, Mr. and Mrs. Simmons, Tony Maretti and John Lovell."

She was examining each of us carefully without any particular interest until she came to John; then her face brightened. "Oh, I know you!" she cried. "You're Alan Westmore in *Stars Away!*"

John said, "That's right."

"What is this — a house party?" she asked Dirk.

He said, "No. We came up to shoot a picture."

"A picture? You mean they are all actors?"

"Yes."

She looked back at John, then went over to him and held out her hands, her multiple bracelets jangling. "This *is* a thrill!" she cried. "I adore you on TV. Everybody does. And to think you're right here in our little town. The girls will be *so* excited. You simply *must* come and talk to us at The Women's Club on Wednesday afternoon."

John had had to stand up and accept the

scrawny hands she'd offered him, but he looked uncomfortable and his face reddened beneath his tan. "I'm afraid I couldn't do that," he said, glancing at Dirk for help.

Dirk suppressed a grin and came into the room. "We are going to have to work every minute for the two weeks we're here," he explained. "I'm afraid no one can goof off."

John managed to get his hands away from Emma Halburton, and she swung around to face Dirk. "Oh, Dirk!" she cried. "You can't be such a slave driver! The girls will all descend on you *en masse* if you don't let this lovely boy come to us."

"Heaven forbid!" Dirk said. Then, "I'm sorry I can't be more hospitable, Emma, but we have to get to work, if you'll excuse us."

The smile left her face, and her bracelets jangled. "Which one is Vicki?" she asked, looking accusingly at me and Ada.

Dirk said, "She isn't here."

"Where is she?"

"I don't know, Emma. Please, I can't talk to you now."

She turned and looked at John, then at Tony. "With such attractive *young* men right here in the house with her, I can't for the life of me understand why she would make a pass at my old Harvey."

Dirk glared at her. "What do you mean by that?" he demanded.

Her lips tightened. "Didn't you know? She

kept him out until five o'clock this morning."

If a pail of cold water had been thrown in his face, Dirk couldn't have looked more surprised. When he could catch his breath, he asked, "Who told you that?"

Emma tossed her head. "*He* did. Harvey. He came in with blonde hairs all over his coat and lipstick on his collar."

Dirk stared at her. His hands were clenched and there was a whiteness around his mouth. "Please get out of here, Emma, or I won't be responsible for what I do."

She seemed surprised at his violent reaction. "If you don't believe me, ask her." Then she turned and went back to John and put an arm around him, the one with the jangly bracelets. Looking up into his face, she said, "If you won't talk to us at the club, you simply must come for dinner some night."

John looked so baffled and helpless. I almost laughed, but I decided there was only one way to get rid of the woman. Getting up, I went around the table and put an arm around John from the other side. "John never goes anywhere without me," I told Emma, looking across John at her. "You see, we're engaged."

The woman let go of him. "Oh," she said, "I'm sorry. I didn't know."

To my surprise, John put his arms around me and kissed my cheek. Into my ear he whispered, "Thanks, pal."

Emma started for the front door, then turned

around. "Then you must come too," she told me, not too enthusiastically. "What was your name again?"

"Cheryl Daniels." I gave her my best smile, the one I use in TV commercials. And that was a mistake. She did a double take and pointed a finger at me. "I know you too!" she cried. "Cold stopper antihistamine tablets!" She sighed and cocked her head to one side. "Oh dear!" she said, and rolled her eyes ceiling-ward. "This is just too much!"

It had to be at that moment that Vicki came down the stairs. "Good morning, everybody," she said blithely. "Is there any breakfast left?"

Emma Halburton swung around and glared at her. "Are you Vicki?" she demanded.

Behind her back Dirk shook his head at Vicki, but she didn't get the message. With her cute little girl smile she said, "Yes, I'm Vicki. Who are you, if I may ask?"

Emma advanced on her. "You may ask," she told her, "and I'll tell you. I'm Harvey's wife, that's who I am. And you stay away from him or I'll — I'll —" Reaching Vicki, she slapped her stingingly across the face, the multiple bracelets jangling like a string of Sarna bells. "I'll give you worse than that!" she finished. Then she turned, opened the front door and stalked out of the house. Dirk caught the door just in time to keep it from slamming.

Vicki stood there holding a hand to her red-dening cheek. There were tears in her eyes.

Dirk went to her and put his arms around her, and John and I, suddenly becoming conscious of each other, separated and couldn't meet each other's eyes.

Chapter Five

By the time Ada and I had the breakfast dishes in the dishwasher, it was ten-thirty. While we were in the kitchen, Dirk took Vicki into the living room and had a quiet, fatherly talk with her. Tony and John were in the dining room going over the equipment; loading the camera with film, the tape recorder with a fresh roll of tape. Later the film and tape would be synchronized.

When Dirk got us all together out on the terrace with our scripts, he arranged chairs in a semicircle, then sat facing us at a folding card table. As soon as we were settled we began a run-through of the play. It sounded flat as we read our parts in a monotone, but we all felt it had something and as we began to memorize our lines it would come to life.

It was about a marriage that was slowly disintegrating for want of communication between the husband and wife. Not a new theme, but I couldn't help wondering if Dirk had based it on his own marriage. I was playing the wife and John the husband. Vicki was the wife's friend who was trying very hard to get the husband on the rebound. Ada was the husband's mother and Charlie the wife's father. They were both trying to save the marriage because both of theirs had ended in divorce. Dirk was Vicki's boy friend and appeared only in the beginning and near the end.

When we'd read through the script once, Dirk said, "Now then, what I want from all of you is your best. We've never worked together before, but we all know each other's work."

We all nodded, and I noticed Vicki looked quite subdued. She also looked tired. Dirk said, "Shall we go through just the first act again? This time try it with a little more feeling."

The play began with the husband and wife having an argument as they came in from an evening party.

It was going to be embarrassing for me to work with John, especially after what had taken place when Emma Halburton was there.

Dirk said, "Okay, Cheryl, you begin." I started guiltily, realizing everybody was waiting for me to read my lines and I'd been staring at a robin who was hopping along the edge of the empty pool.

The scene began at a low level, with the husband and wife arguing about something that had happened at the party from which they had just returned.

As we read our lines, I could feel John's magnetism and instinctively began to fight against it. Dirk, being an astute director, sensed it and said, "Don't fight him so hard right in the beginning, Cheryl. Start in a lower key and build up to the climax at the end of the first act."

I said, "All right. Could we take it from page five?"

In the middle of the first act the husband tries to pacify his irate wife by attempting to make love to her. He tries to take her into his arms and finally succeeds, but when he starts to kiss her she fights him. It would be a good scene when it was acted out, but in a reading it was flat.

One speech of John's was, "Kiss me, damn it! You're still my wife."

And I said, "But not for much longer, believe me!"

Just then we heard footsteps coming along the flagstones at the side of the house, and a man in his late forties, tall, sinewy and deeply tanned, came onto the terrace. He was wearing dungarees and a sweat shirt. Dirk jumped up to greet him. "Joe!" he said. "You got here quickly."

The man said, "Good to see you, Dirk. Thought I'd stop on my way home to lunch and see what you want done. Can't do anything today because I'm working for Mrs. Halburton, but I could come here first thing in the morning."

Dirk said, "Fine," and he and Joe left the terrace and went over to the pool. As they walked away, the man called Joe asked, "What did you do to Mrs. Halburton? She's mad as a wet hen." They were gone only a few minutes, and when Joe left Dirk took his place at the table.

"Now then, Cheryl," he said, "you're fighting John too hard. You're having a fight, sure, but you're being too intense about it. You won't have anything to build up to."

John said, "Suppose you let Cheryl and me work it out together, and you go ahead with the rest of the cast."

Dirk said, "Okay. Good idea. You two go inside or somewhere, and we'll work on the scene with Vicki and me."

John and I got up, and John said, "Let's go into the dining room."

I followed him in, and we sat down side by side at the table. John lit a cigarette, then looked at me speculatively. After a moment he said, "I know you don't like me, Cheryl, but why not let bygones be bygones?"

I felt my face flush. "That's what I thought I was doing."

He blew smoke ceilingward. "No, you're not. I can feel the antagonism. It's in the air between us like an electric current."

I looked down at my script. "Sorry."

He tilted his chair back and hooked his left thumb in his belt. "I've seen you in the TV commercials," he said. "You've improved. You've got something. I don't know how to express it, but it's a certain warmth, charm, magnetism — whatever you want to call it. It comes across on the screen. If you'd only relax and be yourself now. I won't bite you. Don't be afraid of me." He smiled, and a twinkle came into his deep blue eyes.

I rolled up my script, then smoothed it out. My hands were shaking a little.

"Just forget we used to be in love. That's all in the past." He kept looking at me. "Or is it?" he asked.

I jumped up, walked over to a window and stood looking out at cars passing on the lower road. I had my back to John, and for a long time he didn't speak or move.

I whirled around. "John!" I said. I hadn't heard him get up from his chair, but when I turned there he was, so close to me I bumped into him. An, "Oh!" escaped me. Then his arms were around me and his lips were on mine, hard, demanding. I closed my eyes and felt myself go limp. It had never been that good when we were engaged. My arms went up around his neck, and we clung together hungrily while thrill after thrill went through me.

"So this is what you call working it out together?"

The magic of the moment was shattered, and we let each other go. Vicki was standing in the center hall glaring at us. "That ought to look good on a vista vision screen," she said, her teeth clenched. Then to me, "You work fast, don't you? But it won't work any better the second time than it did the first."

I sighed, and quick tears of embarrassment sprang to my eyes. Without answering her, I walked over, sat down at the table and opened my script.

John asked, "Were you looking for us, Vicki?"

She said, "Yes. Dirk wants you. Cheryl and I have a scene together, and later you and I have a scene together."

Seemingly unperturbed, John said, "Okay. Let's go, Cheryl." He picked up his script from the table, strode into the hall and shoved Vicki ahead of him towards the terrace door. I trailed behind them, wishing I were anywhere else but where I was.

When we got back to the terrace, Dirk was telling Tony, "When we get the pool filled, we can do the party scene. I hope the weather holds."

Vicki, John and I sat down in our chairs. Dirk asked, "Got things straightened out?"

I said, "I guess so."

John said, "Oh yes." He smiled at me in an intimate way, and as I met his deep blue eyes I couldn't help wondering if he thought all he had to do was kiss me and erase all the bitterness that had been between us for the last two years.

Fortunately, Vicki kept still.

For the next couple of hours we rehearsed like the professionals we were, putting aside our personal feuds and giving Dirk the best we had. He was such a good director he managed to get the first act whipped into shape, and by the time he called for a break we all knew our lines, and even John and I had taken on the personalities of the characters we were playing and submerged our own personalities into those of Deborah and Allister.

Dirk asked, "Suppose we have some sandwiches and coffee? We can have them out here. The sun doesn't get around here until around two."

I said, "I'll fix the sandwiches." I got up and started across the terrace toward the door into the hall, but as I passed Vicki she stuck out a foot and tripped me. I went flying and flopped on my face. My forehead hit a flagstone, and for a moment I couldn't move. Then Dirk, Tony, Charlie and John were all helping me to my feet, asking, "Cheryl, what happened? Are you all right?"

When I could speak, I didn't know what to say. If I told the truth, it would only cause a row, and things were complicated enough without that. So I said, "I guess I tripped." I felt of my forehead and winced. I'd given it a good bump, and one of my wrists hurt.

Ada came to me and said, "Come upstairs and let me put something on your forehead. You don't want it to discolor or swell, or you won't be able to do the picture."

Dirk said, "God, no!"

So I let Ada lead me inside and upstairs to my room. When we got there I sat down on Vicki's bed and held onto my wrist. Ada asked, "Did you hurt your wrist too?"

I said, "Yes, I guess I put out that hand when I fell."

"Come into the bathroom and we'll bathe it with cold water."

So I went into the bathroom and sat down on a stool, and Ada held a cold wet towel to my head, rewetting it frequently to keep it cold, while I held my wrist under cold running water.

After a few minutes Ada said, "I couldn't be sure, but I thought I saw Vicki stick her foot out just as you passed her."

"She did. But I didn't like to say so and cause a row."

"I know what you mean, but you're going to have to watch that girl. It's too bad you're in the same room with her. I wouldn't trust her any farther than I could throw a battleship."

I turned my wrist over so the cold water could reach the other side. "Oh, she's just a mixed up kid," I said. "She isn't lethal."

"She's a menace! Did you know she and Tony were married once?"

I almost jumped off the stool and splashed water all over myself. "No!" I cried. "When?"

"About five years ago. They were both very young; she was only seventeen and he was twenty. And it only lasted two weeks. They were in a show up in Canada. A friend of mine was in the same show. By the time the company got back to New York, they had split up."

My wrist was beginning to feel better, and I

reached for a towel and dried it. "Poor Tony," I said. "So that's the reason he never gets mixed up with any special girl. I wonder if they're divorced."

"Yes, they are. Tony went down to Mexico and got it. But don't say anything. Maybe I shouldn't have told you."

"I'm glad you did. I wonder if Dirk knows."

"I'm sure he doesn't. Only a few people know, and I'm sure they have forgotten. It was such a short-lived affair. I sometimes wonder if they remember it themselves."

"I'm sure Tony does," I said.

By the time we got downstairs, the boys had made coffee and a plate of sandwiches and had put a cloth on the card table out on the terrace.

Tony said, "Cheryl, you stretch out in this beach chair, and we'll all wait on you. We can't have our leading lady incapacitated." He put a sandwich on a paper plate, along with a triangularly folded paper napkin, and brought it to me. John poured and fixed my coffee. I was touched that he remembered how I liked it: half a lump of sugar and just a dash of cream. When he gave me the cup our eyes met. "I hope you still like it this way," he said quietly, so only I could hear him. I said, "Yes, I do. Thank you."

He touched my forehead with gentle fingers. "That's swelled a little," he said. "I'll get you some ice to hold up to it." He went into the kitchen and in a moment returned with a couple of ice cubes wrapped in a clean dish towel. "Hold this to your forehead," he said. So I put the sandwich plate on my lap, the coffee cup on the arm of the chair, and did as he told me. I was embarrassed to have my eyes fill with tears as I looked up at him and said, "Thanks." But he pretended not to notice. He turned and got himself a sandwich and some coffee and sat down on the far side of the terrace.

We worked steadily all afternoon, and I held ice to my head whenever I could. Dirk, Vicki and the Simmons' were in the first act only briefly, but John and I were on stage constantly.

As the scenes took shape, I found myself feeling more friendly toward John. I had to admit he could act, and I could feel his growing respect for my work. Dirk was pleased with us.

Our dinner was very sketchy, because Dirk wanted to start shooting as soon as it got dark. When I went upstairs to dress in the evening gown required for the next scene, I realized no one had made his bed. I smoothed up mine and Vicki's and then showered and dressed.

I'd brought a floor-length avocado green chiffon evening dress to wear and a darker green velvet waist length cape, and I took particular care with my hair. My only jewelry was going to be a large glittering pin and long heavy dangling earrings.

The dress wasn't new, but fortunately it still looked in style. I'd worn it the last time John and I had gone out together, on the evening when we'd had our final row. Now, as I stood before the mirror screwing on my earrings, I wondered if it had been a good choice. It might remind John of that unpleasant evening.

Fortunately, the swelling on my forehead had gone down enough for me to cover it with makeup, and I was able to bring my hair down to shade it.

Vicki's part didn't call for an evening dress. She and Dirk were supposed to be just driving by the house and to have come in on the spur of the moment. They were to wear sport clothes.

Vicki came upstairs to dress just as I was leaving the room. She brushed by me without speaking, and I decided to let it go at that. However, I didn't look forward to spending the night in the same room with her.

When I went downstairs, Tony was alone in the living room, working with his lights. The camera was set in a position to get John and me as we entered the front door and came into the living room, arguing as we came.

Tony asked, "Where's Vicki?"

I said, "She just went upstairs to change."

Tony came over to inspect my makeup and costume. After a careful check he said, "Okay. Just let's move this piece of hair over that bump. It's swelled a little." He rearranged my hair to his satisfaction, then said, "I saw what happened this morning."

"Oh? What?"

He sat down on the arm of the sofa and leaned an arm across the back. "I saw Vicki trip you."

"It was an accident, I'm sure," I lied.

His lips tightened. "No, it wasn't." He drew in a deep breath and held it a moment before he let it out. Then he said, "You see, I know Vicki. She'll stop at nothing to get her own way."

"But what does she want? Does she want to have my part in the picture?"

To my surprise, Tony said, "She wants *me*, Cheryl."

I stared at him. "But I thought —"

He met my eyes sadly. "You thought she was after John. But she isn't. That's just a smoke screen. She wants *me* back."

I didn't say anything, because Ada had asked me not to mention what she'd told me. Then Tony said, "Nobody knows this, but Vicki and I were married one time — for about two weeks."

I said, "Oh?" and tried to look surprised.

He got up and began pacing back and forth. "Yes," he said. "And it was two weeks of hell. I wouldn't go through it again for anything."

"Didn't you love her?"

He swung around and came toward me. His hands were rammed in his trouser pockets. "Yes, I loved her," he said, his jaw tense and a pulse jumping in his left temple. "I still love her. But I don't *like* her. She's not a nice person."

"Then how can you love her?"

He looked at me for a long moment, then smiled sadly. "That's something I can't explain," he said.

The look in his eyes wrenched my heart, and I couldn't help reaching out a hand to him and patting his cheek. "I'm sorry," I said, and kissed him fleetingly, but not fleetingly enough. Vicki's voice said angrily, "Stay away from him!"

I whirled around, and there she was, standing like an avenging angel in the doorway. She had on a white pleated mini-skirt and a white turtle-necked sweater and her brown eyes were flashing, her hands clenched at her sides. "Stay away from him!" she repeated with ominous quietude, "or so help me, I'll *kill* you!"

I glanced quickly at Tony and saw that his face had paled beneath his tan. "Stop it, Vicki," he said sternly. "Just stop it! If you don't, I won't have you in the show!"

At that, she too turned pale, and for a tense moment I didn't know what she was going to do. Then suddenly she laughed. "You're such a ham, Tony dear," she said, coming into the room. "But really, darling, this isn't an off Broadway melodrama."

I saw Tony forcibly release his tension; then he shrugged and went out onto the terrace, where everybody else was. Not wanting any more words with Vicki, I followed him.

Chapter Six

In spite of the various unpleasantnesses of the day, the filming of the first act went very well, with the exception of the several times we had to stop and redo a scene because of traffic noises down on the road. Twice the fire apparatus clanged by, and several times cars passed filled with screeching teen-agers that sounded like wild Indians on the warpath.

"Is it usually as noisy as this in the evenings?" Tony asked Dirk.

"No, it isn't," Dirk said.

Tony quirked an eyebrow. "Do you think it could be deliberate?"

"I could very easily think that," Dirk said grimly.

"But the fire apparatus?"

"That too. Harvey is a volunteer fireman. They are all friends of his."

Tony shrugged and reset the tape. "This will have to be very carefully edited when we get through," he said. "A normal amount of traffic noise would be all right, but not this much."

It was after midnight when we got through, and everyone was exhausted. Surprisingly, Vicki had behaved very well all evening and had kept her feelings toward Tony and me well under control. But I still didn't look forward to sleeping in the same room with her.

Charlie suggested, "Why don't we go somewhere for hamburgers?" but Dirk said, "No place open. Everything around here closes down at nine o'clock. But we can raid the refrigerator. There's coke and beer and sandwich makings; maybe a few hamburgers."

During the move to the kitchen, Tony took me out on the terrace. "Cheryl, I'm worried about you," he said.

"Oh? Why?"

"I don't think it's a good idea for you and Vicki to share the same room."

It was delightfully cool out on the terrace, and the symphony of the night insects was pleasant to hear. I would have liked to sit out there for a while and unwind before going to bed, but Tony and I both knew we had better not let ourselves be missed. I said, "I don't like it much myself, but I don't believe she'd dare try anything."

Tony lit a cigarette, and it glowed in the darkness. "You can't count on that. I'm going to suggest John and I take the big room, and you and Vicki take our rooms. You'll still have to share a bathroom with Vicki, but you can lock your door while you're sleeping."

"Well, if you can arrange it without causing any more trouble."

"I'll do that. And to be perfectly honest, I have a double reason for the change. If I'm in a room alone, she may try to come see me sometime."

"Oh, she wouldn't do that!"

"You don't know her."

Dirk came out with a bottle of beer. "Hey, don't you two want something to eat or drink?" he said, collapsing in one of the beach chairs. "God, I'm beat!" He sighed.

Tony said, "Me too. Any more beer left?"

Dirk said, "Sure, if you move fast enough. We'll have to drive over to a supermarket tomorrow and stock up for the weekend."

I went into the house and joined the rest of the gang in the kitchen. Ada was grilling hamburgers, and they smelled heavenly. Charlie and John were laughing at a story Vicki was telling, and Tony had just come into the kitchen behind me, when a shot was heard. We all jumped and looked questioningly at each other. Then I cried, "Dirk!" and ran out to the terrace.

Dirk was standing at the edge of the terrace with a smoking gun in his hand. "What is it?" I asked.

Still looking out at the darkness, Dirk said, "Somebody took a shot at me."

"But *you* have a gun?"

"Yes, luckily."

"We only heard *one* shot."

"He had a silencer on his."

"Maybe it was someone hunting? Do they hunt around here at night?"

"Just occasionally, to chase a racoon away from a garbage can. And then they'd use a rifle, not a gun with a silencer on it."

"But who — ?"

John and Tony came out. "Are you all right?" they asked in unison.

"Yes. He missed me. The bullet hit that peach tree at the end of the terrace. Missed my head by about an inch."

I shuddered, thinking of Helen and the little boy down in New York.

Charlie came out in time to hear the conversation. "Do you always pack a gun when you're up here?" he asked.

Dirk shook his head. "No. I found this in Aunt Suzy's knitting basket and decided my pocket was a better place for it."

Vicki came out, drinking from a coke bottle. "I thought you said your aunt was a sweet little old lady."

Dirk gave up his search of the shadows and sank down in a wicker chair. "She was."

"Then why should she have a gun hidden in her knitting basket?"

"That's what I'd like to know," Dirk said, looking down at the gun in his hands. "She must have been afraid of something or somebody."

Without realizing I was going to speak, I asked, "Of Harvey?"

He glanced up at me. His face was drawn, and he looked awfully tired. "If I thought that,"

71

he said, his teeth clenched, "I'd —"

John took the gun from his hands and put it in the pocket of his tuxedo coat. "Maybe we'd all better go into the house and lock the doors," he said.

Without answering him, we all did as he suggested, and Dirk went around the first floor locking doors and windows. Then we congregated in the kitchen again, but by that time nobody wanted the hamburgers Ada had cooked. I said, "Never mind. I can make a meat loaf of them tomorrow."

"Shouldn't you call the police?" Ada asked Dirk.

He said, "No. That wouldn't do any good."

The men finished their beer and smoked cigarettes, and Ada and I quickly cleaned up the kitchen so it wouldn't be in a mess in the morning. I was beginning to wonder how Tony was going to manage the switch of rooms when he said, "Hey, Dirk, I was thinking, maybe the girls would rather have the separate rooms. Why don't John and I change with them? You wouldn't mind bunking with me, would you, John?"

John looked surprised but said, "No. Whatever the girls want to do."

Watching Vicki, I saw her lips tighten. "Suppose we don't want to switch?" she said, almost too sweetly.

Tony put his empty beer bottle in the sink. "Sure you do," he said. "Girls always like to have rooms to themselves." He started for the door to the hall. "Come on. We'll move the stuff now."

John put his beer bottle in the sink and followed Tony, and I said, "Come on, Vicki. You'll sleep better by yourself. I'm restless, and the cat sleeps with me."

"Cat?" she cried. "I haven't seen any cat."

I went out into the hall, opened the door to the terrace and called, "Here, Kitty, Kitty, Kitty," and in a moment Tommy came bounding onto the terrace and into the house with his long, silky black tail waving aloft. He had something in his mouth, and I leaned down and took it. It was a gold chain bracelet with charms hanging from it, and it reminded me of the one Emma Halburton had been wearing that morning. I closed my hand around it. If I showed it to Dirk, he'd probably go right over to Harvey's and Emma's with the gun. And I couldn't believe that Emma Halburton would be prowling around at midnight shooting at people with a gun that had a silencer on it. I shut and locked the door, slipped the bracelet down the front of my dress and returned to the kitchen. The cat followed me, and I broke up one of the hamburgers on a saucer and put it on the floor for him. He made short work of it and looked up at me gratefully, so I gave him a saucer of milk. Dirk said, "You seem to have made a friend."

"I've always liked cats," I said.

Vicki tossed back her long, straight platinum

hair. "That's understandable," she said.

I clenched my teeth but managed to keep my mouth shut. Dirk said, "You girls go on upstairs and get your things moved, and I'll finish up down here and put out the lights."

By the time we got upstairs, John and Tony had all their things in our room. They didn't have much; just a suitcase apiece.

Vicki began throwing her things into her suitcase with evident dissatisfaction, but the boys didn't seem to notice, and I tried to avoid her as we went back and forth carrying things to the other rooms. I let her choose which room she wanted, although there really wasn't any choice. They were both attractive and spacious enough for one person. She chose the one Tony had had, and so I began hanging my clothes in the closet of the room John had slept in last night.

By the time we were settled in our new quarters, Ada and Charlie had gone to their room and their door was closed. The rest of us called good night to one another, and Dirk went into his room and closed the door. Vicki and I each closed our hall doors, but the doors leading into the connecting bath were still open, and there was a light on in the bathroom. I called to Vicki, "Do you want to use the bathroom first?"

She called, "Yes, I do," so I closed the door on my side and began getting undressed. When I took off my bra, the bracelet fell to the floor with a little tinkle. I picked it up and examined it under the light of a strong reading lamp. The charms were the usual type: a heart, a key, a gold silhouette of a child's head on which was engraved, Billy, March 6, 1967, something that resembled the Greek letters of a fraternity emblem and a disk shaped like a wedding cake on which was engraved, Helen and Dirk, June 3, 1966. My heart gave a jump. That was the date of Dirk's wedding. But why would Emma Halburton be wearing a disk like that on her charm bracelet? I put the bracelet into my purse and put my purse into a drawer in the bureau. I'd try to question Dirk tomorrow about the disk. I'd have to do it discreetly, of course, but I simply had to know.

When Vicki finished in the bathroom, she didn't bother to tell me. I just heard her slam the door on her side. So I went in and started to run the shower. But just as I was about to step into the tub I looked down and saw several pieces of jagged broken glass on the rubber mat, right where I was about to step. When I returned to my room, I carefully locked my door.

I'd just gotten into bed when I heard Tommy jumping at a door; probably Dirk's, where I had been the night before. I got up, unlocked my hall door and looked out. The hall was dark, but I could see someone standing outside Dirk's door. I couldn't be sure, but it looked like a woman with long skirts or a long cloak or negligee. Then, as my eyes became accustomed to the dark, I could see two luminous yellow eyes looking up at the woman. Apprehensively I called softly, "Tommy?" and the cat turned his head and looked at me. Then he made a leap in the air and raced toward me, rushing past me into my room. I had taken my eyes from the woman outside Dirk's door only for a split-second, but when I looked back at her she was gone. But where? Dirk's door hadn't opened, nor had any of the other doors, and there was no one in the hall or on the stairs.

I closed my door and locked it and snapped on an overhead ceiling light that connected with the switch beside the door, to see where Tommy was. He was on the bed, standing with his back arched and his tail twice the normal size. Every hair on his body seemed to be standing out as if wired. His eyes were enormous with fright. I went over and sat down on the bed beside him, and he jumped at me and put his two front paws on my shoulders, his claws grabbing at my bare shoulders, his head nestled beneath my chin. I put my arms around him and held him close to me and could feel him trembling. I began smoothing his back and talking to him. "It's all right, Tommy. Nice kitty. Take it easy. There, there, nice kitty." After a few minutes he stopped trembling, but he kept hanging onto me and rubbing his head against my face. When I was sure he had quieted down, I got up and snapped off the light, still keeping him in my arms; then I went back to the bed and let him lie close to me beneath the covers, and gradually he began to purr.

Who or what had been out in the hall I dared not surmise. Dirk had said he wouldn't be afraid of Aunt Suzy's ghost, but I wasn't so sure I wouldn't be.

I was awakened by Joe Hinkley working in the pool. It was eight o'clock. I got up and looked out the window. Joe was cleaning out the broken twigs and dead leaves that had accumulated during the winter and whistling the tune to the Salem cigarette commercial.

Tommy got up from the foot of the bed, yawned, stretched and jumped off the bed. Then he went to the hall door and looked up at me. I let him out, and he shot off.

Afterwards, while I was dressing, there was no sound of Vicki using the bathroom. I put on a pair of navy slacks and a pink tailored blouse with a buttoned breast pocket and tied a navy scarf around my neck, tucking the ends into the front of the blouse. Then I took the charm bracelet and put it into the breast pocket of my blouse and buttoned the flap, making sure the bracelet didn't show through the material. I slipped my feet into sneakers, and before leaving the room I made my bed.

When I got downstairs Dirk had the coffee perking. He said, "We'd better do our marketing right after breakfast so we can get to work as early as possible."

"Can't we make a list and just a couple of us go? Then the others can be rehearsing or studying their lines. It will save a little time."

Dirk said, "Good idea. Why don't you and John go? I can work with Vicki and the Simmons' while you're gone."

I didn't much like the idea of going alone with John, but I didn't want to say so.

We decided on cold cereal for breakfast, along with orange juice, toast and coffee. Vicki was the last one down. She breezed into the dining room dressed in light blue shorts and a white cotton turtle-necked, sleeveless sweater. With a blithe, "Good morning, everybody," she sat down in the vacant chair which was between Ada and Dirk. I was sitting across the table between John and Tony. She pretended she didn't see me.

John said to Dirk, "You'd better tell me how to get to the supermarket. You know I'm a stranger in these parts."

Vicki perked up. "Somebody going somewhere?" she asked.

Dirk said, "John and Cheryl are going to do the marketing. We're running out of food."

She bounded on her chair like a child. "Oh! I want to go too."

Dirk said, "You're going to stay here and rehearse."

She gave him an impish grin. "Oh, no, I'm not," she said. "I'm not going to let Cheryl have John all to herself like that."

John smiled slightly. "I don't think I'll need any protection in the supermarket."

Suddenly I remembered Emma's reaction to him yesterday. "Oh goodness!" I cried. "Yes you will too."

He grinned. "Now don't tell me you are planning on seducing me in Aisle Three, between the canned soups and the detergents."

I laughed. "No. I promise. But if we should meet Emma Halburton or any of her girl friends from the Women's Club, I'm not sure I could protect you."

Everybody laughed. That is, everybody but Vicki. She said, "Why don't Tony and I go? We're not celebrities — yet."

I glanced at Ada appealingly, and she said, "Why not let Charlie and me go? We're old hands at the battle of the supermarket."

Dirk looked relieved. "Good idea," he said. "Have you a driver's license, Charlie?"

Charlie said, "No. But Ada has."

I wanted to be alone with Dirk so I could question him about the charm bracelet. So I said, "Dirk, why don't you and I go? Tony can take over the rehearsals. He's done a lot of directing."

Dirk thought a moment, then shrugged. "Well, maybe that would be best. But let's get going right away. Ada and Vicki can clean up the breakfast dishes."

Vicki began to pout. "Oh, Dirk, you know

I'm just no good in a kitchen."

Tony lit a cigarette, and as he was shaking out the match he said, "Then it's time you learned to be. You're a big girl now."

Vicki gave him a startled look, and for a moment I was afraid there was going to be an explosion. But all she said was, "Listen to Father Time."

Tony's lips tightened. "You listen to me, sister!" he said. "You do your share here or you'll get shipped back home."

She tossed her head defiantly. "Isn't that Dirk's prerogative?" she asked.

Dirk pushed his chair back from the table and stood up. "Tony and I are in this together," he said. "So be a good girl and cooperate."

She frowned, pouted, then shrugged. "Oh, all right," she said. "So I'll be a galley slave."

John rose and picked up his soiled dishes to carry them into the kitchen. "Save the dramatics for rehearsal time," he said, and strode into the kitchen.

Vicki balled her paper napkin and threw it angrily at her dish of corn flakes. She hadn't eaten anything. "I seem to be as popular around here as a case of smallpox!" she cried, jumping up.

Quietly Ada said, "Perhaps your popularity is only exceeded by your childishness."

Vicki glared at her. "You too?" she snapped.

Ada smiled and nodded. "Me too, when you deserve it." She rose and began gathering up dishes. "Now come on, let's get these out of the way. The terrace looks very inviting this morning."

Dirk beckoned to me, and I said, "Just a minute until I get my purse."

And I went upstairs.

Chapter Seven

As soon as Dirk and I were on our way to the supermarket I asked, "Dirk, did you notice those bracelets Emma Halburton had on yesterday?"

"Not especially. She always has something jingling on her."

"Well, I suppose a man wouldn't notice, but one of her bracelets was a charm bracelet. That's a chain that has small things attached to it; like hearts or keys or other miniatures."

Dirk said, "I know what you mean. Helen has one. I've given her a couple of things for it. And that reminds me. She wanted me to have it made smaller for her, and I forgot all about it."

I said, "Oh, what things did you get for her?"

He turned the car onto a main highway, and as soon as he was in the stream of traffic he said, "Well, I got her a heart and had our names and the date we got engaged engraved on it. There's a little jewelry shop on Lexington Avenue that makes a specialty of things like that. And I got her a miniature of my frat pin."

My heart began to pound, and I felt as if the bracelet in the pocket of my blouse must surely make itself known. I even put a hand on the pocket to be sure it was there. It was. I asked,

"Is that all she has on hers so far?"

Dirk passed a slow moving car. "No. She sent to one of those mail order places for the silhouette of a child's head and had the name *Billy* and his birth date engraved on it."

"It must be cute," I said. My voice shook a little.

Dirk said, "Yes, it is. She says if we have any more children she'll have one made for each one."

"I suppose Emma's charms are entirely different."

"I should think so. There would be no reason for her to have the same things Helen has."

I didn't answer that. What else was there to say? Undoubtedly the bracelet I had in my pocket belonged to Dirk's wife, Helen.

Just as Dirk was pulling into the parking lot of the supermarket, I asked, "Was Helen up here last summer?"

Dirk stopped the car between two white lines, turned off the ignition, took out the keys and put them into his pocket. "She came up to Aunt Suzy's funeral."

"Has she had her bracelet since then?"

He had opened the car door and was about to get out. But at my question he stopped, turned and looked at me and said, "Of course. Why?"

"I was just wondering."

"You don't think the bracelet Emma had on was Helen's, do you?"

"No. I just wondered." I opened the car door beside me and started to get out, but Dirk grabbed my arm. "Wait a minute," he said. "What are you getting at?"

"Nothing."

"You must have *some* reason for all these questions. It isn't like you to talk about trivial things like charm bracelets."

I sat very still, wondering what to say. If the bracelet I had in my pocket belonged to Helen, then she had been out there in the shadows back of the terrace last night. But why? Was she spying on Dirk? Did she want to get something on him so she could divorce him? Would she have come all the way from the city to shoot him? It seemed unlikely. As far as I knew, there was nothing wrong between Dirk and Helen. But if she was up here, why didn't she make herself known? And where was she staying? If I gave Dirk the bracelet I had in my pocket, what would he do?

He was still holding my arm and watching my face. "Why are you trembling?" he asked, and there was the suggestion of a smile on his lips. I hadn't realized I was trembling until he mentioned it. But why should he think it amusing? Then it suddenly dawned on me. He thought I was trembling because of his nearness and because his hand was holding my arm. "Oh! For heaven sakes!" I cried, and yanked my arm away. He chuckled, and we both got out of the car.

As we walked across the parking lot, I knew my face must be a bright pink.

In the store we each took a cart. We had a long list of things to buy and it was going to be more than one cart could hold. It was an enormous store. The supermarkets in the country are much larger than the ones we have in the city.

It was at the dairy case that we met Emma. "Oh, there you are," she said brightly. "I phoned you, and one of your friends said you'd come over here."

Dirk said, "Yes."

Emma had on all of her bracelets again, and I carefully noticed one of them was a charm bracelet but not at all like the one I had in my pocket. She said, "Harvey wants you to stop in the bank and have a talk with him. I know it's Saturday, but he went in anyway."

Dirk picked up two boxes of eggs. "I haven't anything to talk to Harvey about, and I'm much too busy. I'm sorry, Emma."

Emma's bright look disappeared, and her eyes became sharp, her lips thin and tight. "You're making a mistake, Dirk," she said. "You can't treat Harvey like that!"

Dirk began collecting quart containers of milk and a pint of cream. "Perhaps Harvey doesn't realize he can't order me around?"

I picked up a pound of butter and put it in my cart; then I asked Dirk, "Any cheese?"

He said, "Yes. Get a box of the cheddar." So

I took one and put it in my cart.

Emma said, "You're just being vindictive, Dirk. You don't really want that big house. You wouldn't leave the city and live up here."

He looked down at her. Their eyes met, and I felt I wanted to get out of the way. "But I do want it," he said. "And I intend to keep it for vacations and for when I retire. So you might as well give up."

Emma jingled her bracelets and tossed her head, said an angry, "Oh!" and walked away.

I didn't say anything until Dirk did. "I suppose you're wondering what that was all about?" he said.

"It's none of my business."

We strolled up one aisle and down another, taking the things we needed and putting them in the carts. After a moment Dirk said, "Harvey and Emma want me to sell them the house."

"Don't they have a house of their own?"

"Yes, but it isn't as big or as nice as Aunt Suzy's. Hers was always known as the Manor House. That is to say, it was the largest house in the village years ago."

"Does Harvey want the place badly enough to shoot you for it?"

He said, "Ssshhh! She may be in the next aisle."

"I'm sorry."

"That's all right." Then in a low tone of voice, "That wouldn't get it for him, because if anything happens to me, everything I have goes to Helen."

I thought that over for a while, inadvertently put my hand on my blouse pocket and decided I'd better keep still.

As we were driving back to the house, Dirk said, "I'll take you past Harvey's place." Which he did, on our way to the village. Harvey's place was a small white clapboard house that appeared to have about seven rooms. There was a large lawn with enormous old shade trees and a two-car garage. I said, "It looks like a nice place."

Dirk said, "It is. But Harvey always thought he was going to get Aunt Suzy's house."

"Do they have any children?"

"No."

The bank was on the main street of the village, and just as we were passing it Harvey came out. He had his left arm in a sling. Dirk slowed the car and called to him, "What did you do to your arm?"

Harvey stopped and looked around. When he saw who it was, he came toward the car. "Broke it," he said. "Fell off a ladder last night."

Dirk said, "That's too bad." Then, "We just met Emma in the supermarket."

Harvey said, "Did you? Did she tell you I wanted to have a talk with you?"

"Yes, she did. But I won't have time. They're waiting for me to get back to start rehearsals."

Harvey's eyes narrowed. "Is Helen coming

up?" he asked, and looked at me significantly.

Dirk said, "No. Not this time."

Harvey put his right hand to his left shoulder as if it hurt him. "Thought I saw her this morning," he said.

Dirk shook his head. "No. She's down in the city in the apartment. Next week she may go to Rye and visit her mother until I get back." He raced the car motor, and Harvey stepped back. Dirk raised a hand in salute, called, "See you around," and drove on. His hands were gripping the wheel so hard his knuckles were white.

Maybe I shouldn't have said it, but it was out before I realized it. "Do you believe he really broke his arm?"

He gave me a quick glance. "Why shouldn't I?"

"Well, I was thinking — that shot you fired last night — could it have hit someone in the shoulder?"

He jammed his foot on the brake, and the car stopped so suddenly I was thrown forward. If I hadn't had my seat belt fastened, my head would have hit the windshield. It was lucky there wasn't a car behind us, or they'd have rammed us. "If I thought that, I'd — I'd —" He drew in a deep breath and held it until his face began to get red. When he released the breath he said, "As soon as we get back to the house, I'm going to call Helen." He started the car and drove slowly the rest of the way back to the house.

Chapter Eight

When we returned to the house everybody was on the back terrace, but they didn't seem to be doing much rehearsing.

Ada came into the kitchen to help put away the groceries, and Dirk went up to his room to call Helen.

"Everything under control?" I asked Ada.

"On the surface. But Tony is avoiding Vicki."

I put the eggs in the refrigerator. "Tony told me about their marriage last evening."

Ada was taking meat from the plastic packages and rewrapping it in foil. There was a nice steak, lamb chops and several pounds of chopped chuck. "How did that happen?" she asked. So I told her about the scene in the living room, keeping my voice low so those on the terrace wouldn't hear me.

Ada listened, shaking her head and chewing at her lips. "Did she actually say she would kill you if you didn't stay away from Tony?"

I rearranged things on the top shelf so the cartons of milk would fit. "Yes, she did. But I'm sure she didn't mean it literally. She gets excited."

Ada handed me the packages of meat to pack into the freezer. "I think the trip up here was a mistake," she said.

"How does Charlie feel about it?"

"Charlie doesn't feel. Period!" There was such an unhappy expression in her eyes I wanted to put my arms around her, but I knew she wouldn't want sympathy.

I asked, "Isn't he enjoying being in the show?"

She shrugged. "Oh, in a way. But he doesn't actually enjoy anything any more."

"Maybe this trip will change that."

She walked over to the sink and leaned back against it. "I doubt it. But at least he hasn't been drinking since we've been here, except for beer."

I finished putting the things in the refrigerator and closed the door. Then I gathered and stacked the cartons and put them to one side. "We saw Emma and Harvey over in the village," I said.

Ada inspected a broken fingernail. "Oh?"

"Yes. Harvey has his left arm in a sling. He says he broke it falling off a ladder last night."

She gave me a quick look, and I knew she was thinking the same thing I was. After a moment's silence she said, "Tony found a bullet embedded in the trunk of that peach tree at the side of the terrace this morning. He and John dug it out with a knife."

I felt my heart give a jerk. "Oh! What did they do with it?"

"Tony put it in his pocket. He's going to give it to Dirk."

"Who's going to give me what?" Dirk asked, coming into the kitchen. He had a script in his hand. Ada left the support of the sink and turned to face him. "Tony. He found a bullet in that peach tree this morning."

"The one someone shot at me?"

Ada shrugged. "Who knows? Unless you can find the gun it was shot from."

"I doubt if we'll ever do that." Dirk went and looked out of the window above the sink.

"Unless all the houses in the vicinity could be searched," I said.

Dirk shook his head. "We can't do that."

I asked, "Did you get Helen?"

He shook his head again, keeping his back to us. "I got the cleaning woman. She said Mrs. Halburton and the baby had gone out of town for a few days."

"Probably she went up to her mother's."

He shook his head again. "No. I called her. She said Helen had brought the baby up to her, and then she'd borrowed her car to come up here. She was upset when I told her Helen hadn't arrived. She said she'd left there about four o'clock yesterday afternoon."

"Then she should have been here by eight last evening."

"Yes, she should. Or nine anyway."

Ada and I exchanged glances, but neither of us spoke, and Dirk kept standing there with his back to us, looking out the window over the sink.

Inadvertently I felt of the pocket in my

blouse. The charm bracelet was still there. And Harvey had said he thought he'd seen Helen in the village that morning. Could she have stopped at a motel for the night and be arriving at any minute now?

There seemed to be no way to end the silence. Finally Dirk turned around, and there was that white line around his mouth. He heaved a deep sigh, then said, "Well, we'd better get to work."

The three of us walked slowly out of the kitchen onto the terrace. The chair beside John was empty, and one beside Charlie. Ada had left her script in that one when she came in to help me. Now she returned to it, sat down and patted Charlie's hand. That left the chair beside John for me. He asked, "Get us something good to eat?"

I said, "We did our best. But it's all easy to prepare."

John had on navy blue shorts and his long, well shaped, muscular legs were crossed. His shirt was khaki and opened halfway down the front. I had an almost uncontrollable desire to kiss the hollow at the base of his throat. Our eyes met and I saw him catch at a breath. Then he made a quick movement in his chair, dropped his script and leaned over to pick it up. I sat down in the chair beside him and could feel myself blushing. I pretended to fuss with my hair and fervently hoped no one would notice the blush.

Fortunately, just then Joe Hinkley saw Dirk and called to him, and everyone glanced in his direction. Dirk strolled over to the pool. Joe said, "I'll be able to fill this up this afternoon."

Dirk said, "So soon?"

"Sure. I'll scrub it out and fill it and put the chlorine in. You can all have a swim before dinner."

Dirk said, "Good." Then he asked, "How did Harvey break his arm?"

Joe Hinkley looked up from where he was standing in the bottom of the empty pool. "Did he?" he asked. "I ain't seen him today. He was all right yesterday."

Dirk looked at him thoughtfully for a moment, then said, "Well, I'd better get to work." He came back to the terrace and sat down at the card table. "You all got your scripts?" he asked.

I said, "I haven't. It's up on my bureau. I'll go up and get it."

I started to get up, but John put a hand on my arm. "Sit still. I'll get it for you."

He was back in less time than it would have taken me just to get upstairs. When he handed me the script, I said, "Thank you."

He gave me a smile that sent a thrill through me. "Any time," he said, and sat down beside me, managing to shove his chair closer to mine so our arms were touching.

For the next couple of hours Dirk had us all working on the first scene of the second act. It

93

was laid in the bedroom which had been Aunt Suzy's. Deborah and Allister, the roles John and I played, were getting up in the morning, following their evening fracas in the living room. They had scarcely finished dressing when Vicki, who was Rosemary in the play, arrived and burst into the room. There was an argument and Rosemary said she wouldn't leave until Deborah promised to give Allister a divorce. She planked herself down in the rocking chair and rocked vigorously.

The second act was going to take longer to rehearse than the first one had. To begin with, it was longer, in two scenes; one in the bedroom and one in and around the pool. And the speeches were longer.

Vicki couldn't remember her lines, and Dirk worked with her, making her go over and over them until she began to rebel.

Tony, not having a part in the play, left us and strolled across the field. He went as far as the shack that looked like a tool house, walked around it, lifted the latch, opened the door and looked inside. Then he made a leap into the shack. He was inside quite a while, and as Dirk worked with Vicki, I sat watching for him to come out. Being a curious person, I wondered what was inside the shack that had made Tony leap into it so fast. I didn't like to leave the rehearsal and go over to see, because any minute Dirk might want John and me to go over our parts before Vicki, or rather Rosemary, arrived.

Then Tony came out of the shack, put his fingers in his mouth and gave a shrill whistle.

Dirk turned around, and Tony beckoned to him. Dirk cupped his hands to his mouth and yelled, "What do you want?"

Tony cupped his hands to his mouth and yelled, "You! Dirk! Come over here."

Reluctantly Dirk got up and went across the field toward the shack. John said, "Guess I'll go too." I got up to follow, but John said, "Don't you come. You girls stay here. It looks as if something is wrong." He began to run after Dirk, and I went over to the pool. Joe Hinkley was scrubbing the sides with a long-handled brush. I asked, "What's in that shack over there?"

He looked up me. He was at the deep end of the pool, so he couldn't see over the top. "That?" he said. "Nothin' much. A lawn mower, some rakes and hoes and some rope. Stuff like that."

Dirk had reached the shack, and he and Tony went inside. I asked Joe, "Have you been in there this morning?"

He said, "No. I got this stuff from the barn." He indicated the brush and a pail of water. Then he asked, "You swim?"

I said, "Yes." I was watching John reach the shack and go inside. Now the three of them were inside, and they were staying inside. I went back to the terrace. Ada, Charlie and Vicki were watching the shack. "What do you

95

suppose is the matter?" Ada asked.

I said, "I don't know. But John said we'd better stay here."

Crossly Vicki said, "John said! John said! So what? I'm going over." She threw her script onto the card table and started across the field.

Charlie said, "I'm going upstairs and lie down a few minutes. I'm tired."

Ada said, "All right."

After Charlie had gone, Ada and I stood on the terrace side by side. Finally I said, "I wish they'd come out."

"So do I. I'm getting nervous."

Vicki reached the shack and went in, but she came right out and started back across the field, walking quickly.

I couldn't stand it another minute. I left Ada and went to meet Vicki. When I was within talking distance I asked, "What's the matter?"

She looked pale and frightened. All her cockiness was gone. "It's Dirk's wife," she said. "She's in there — tied up and gagged and —"

I ran to her and grabbed her arms. "And what?"

"I don't know. The boys were trying to get her untied."

"She isn't — ?" I couldn't say the word. I left Vicki and began to run across the field. When I reached the shack John was just coming out. "Oh, Cheryl," he said. I'd never seen him look so serious. "Go back to the house and call the doctor. Dirk says his name is in the notebook in the drawer of the bedside table in his room. His name is Doctor Brooks."

I asked, "Is she hurt?"

"I don't think seriously. But she's been hit on the head, and she's lost a lot of blood. I'm going to get one of the beach chairs so we can carry her to the house." He put an arm around my shoulders, and we started back to the house. I knew I was shaking. "Steady now," John said, and his arm around me tightened.

I asked, "How could she have gotten in there?"

"Somebody put her there. She never got there by herself."

I stopped walking. We were still far enough from the terrace so our voices wouldn't be heard. I said, "John, I think I should tell you something."

"What?"

"Last night, when I called the cat in, remember?"

"Yes."

"Well, when he came in he had something in his mouth. I took it from him, and I have it here." With trembling hands I unbuttoned the pocket in my blouse and took out the charm bracelet. John looked at it. "What is it?"

"A charm bracelet."

He touched it with a finger. "Does it belong to that woman who was here yesterday?"

"Emma Halburton? No. It's Helen's."

John stared at me. "But how did the cat get it?"

"He must have found it outside."

John kept looking down at my face, which felt drained of all color. "You think Helen was on the grounds last night?"

"She must have been." Then I cried, "What's going on here?" He put his arms around me, and I leaned my head against his shoulder for a moment. Then I managed to pull myself together, and we went the rest of the way to the house.

By the time we reached the terrace, Vicki had collapsed in one of the beach chairs and Ada was trying to calm her. I didn't stop except to ask Ada, "Did Vicki tell you?"

Ada said, "Yes."

I hurried into the house and up to Dirk's room. The notebook was right where he had said it was, and I called the doctor. Fortunately, it was his office hours and he was there. He said, "I'll be right over."

While I talked to him, I watched the rocking chair. Did it move or didn't it? I couldn't be sure. When I finished the phone call, I went over to the chair and stood in front of it. I wondered what would happen if I sat down in it. But I couldn't bring myself to do so. To be sure, it was broad daylight, and ghosts didn't usually appear in broad daylight. Or did they? I'd never met one, so I didn't know.

I walked across the room to the door, and just as I went into the hall I turned and glanced back at the chair. It was rocking.

I hate to admit this, but I ran all the way down the stairs, my heart racing even faster than my feet. When I went out on the terrace, Tony and John were coming across the field, carrying the beach chair with Helen lying on it. Dirk was walking beside the chair, holding Helen's hand.

Vicki and Ada were sitting at the card table watching the cortege.

As they came onto the terrace, Dirk asked me, "Did you get Doctor Brooks?"

I said, "Yes. He'll be right over."

Helen was lying on the chair with her eyes closed. Her face was narcissus white — waxy white. Her lips seemed bloodless, but there was blood on her face and on one side of her head. Her blonde hair was matted with dried blood, and there was a nasty-looking gash in her scalp.

I asked Dirk, "Had I better go up and open your bed?"

He said, "No. I think we'll have to get her to a hospital."

Helen opened her eyes and looked up appealingly at Dirk. "Stay with you," she murmured.

Dirk managed a smile. "I'll go to the hospital with you. Don't worry now."

Her eyelids closed again, and she seemed to be scarcely breathing.

Dirk said, "We'd better set the chair down here on the terrace until the doctor gets here. I don't think she should be moved any more than necessary." So John and Tony set the chair down gently, and just then we heard a car coming up the driveway at the front of the house.

Dirk asked me, "Will you go meet the doctor, Cheryl, and bring him out here?"

I said, "Sure."

Doctor Brooks was short and paunchy, but he had a round, kindly face and large gray eyes that looked through his dark-rimmed glasses with understanding and compassion.

He followed me through the hall to the terrace, greeted Dirk, then pulled a chair close to Helen and sat down beside her. He put his bag on the flagstones, picked up one of Helen's limp hands and felt of her pulse. Helen opened her eyes and tried to smile at him, but she couldn't manage it. "Doctor Brooks," she murmured, "I got hurt."

He said, "So I see. What were you doing?"

"Nothing."

"Where were you when it happened?"

Her lips tightened. "I don't remember."

"Who hit you?" He was examining her head now, and she flinched.

"I don't know. It was dark. I couldn't see."

Doctor Brooks took his stethoscope from his bag and listened to her heart, and she closed her eyes and lay there as limp as a rag doll.

When the doctor had finished his examination, he said to Dirk, "We'd better get over to the hospital."

Dirk nodded. "Shall I call for an ambulance?"

100

The doctor said, "I will." He stood up. "I know where the phone is."

Dirk said, "There's one on the desk in the living room and one on the wall in the kitchen."

The doctor nodded and went into the house, and we all waited for his return; Ada and Vicki still sitting at the card table and the rest of us standing watching Helen, who now seemed to be unconscious.

I gently urged Dirk into the chair beside Helen in which the doctor had been sitting, and he collapsed onto it.

Ada said, "I'll make some coffee." She got up and went to the kitchen.

When the doctor came back he said, "They'll send an ambulance over in a few minutes." He went to Helen, took her pulse again, then sat down near her to wait for the arrival of the ambulance. Then, as doctors do under conditions of that sort, he attempted to make conversation. "Had your cousin Harvey in the office last night," he told Dirk. "He'd been cleaning his gun, and it went off accidentally. Shot himself in the shoulder. Nothing serious. Just a flesh wound."

Dirk and I looked at each other; then Dirk said, "Oh? I thought he *broke* his arm. Saw him over in the village this morning, and he told me he'd fallen off a ladder and *broken* his arm."

The doctor smiled. "Guess he was kind of ashamed to admit he was stupid enough to clean a loaded gun.'

Dirk leaned over and put his elbows on his spread knees, clasped his hands between them and looked at them thoughtfully. "Um," he said.

I went into the kitchen to help Ada. She had water boiling and was making instant coffee. She said, "I thought this would be better than waiting for the percolator."

I helped her put the cups on a tray with a bowl of sugar and a pitcher of cream, spoons and paper napkins, and carried the tray out to the terrace, selling it on the card table.

Dirk got up and took a cup to the doctor. "Milk and cream?" he asked him.

The doctor said, "No, thank you. I like it black."

The rest of us helped ourselves. I didn't really want any, but I wondered if Joe Hinkley would like a cup. I looked over into the pool, but Joe wasn't there. I asked Vicki, "Where's Joe? Did you see him?"

She said, "He went over to the barn with the pail. I guess he wanted to get some clean water. Or maybe he's gone home for lunch."

The ambulance arrived and Dirk went with Helen, sitting beside her as the ambulance drove away, the doctor following in his car.

After they'd gone, the rest of us sat on the terrace, not saying anything. We were all too shocked and stunned.

As for me, I kept feeling of the pocket of my

blouse, more conscious than ever of the charm bracelet I was carrying there. Whatever would I do with it? Considering the latest happening, I didn't want to give it to Dirk. And I didn't want to dispose of it, because I knew it had sentimental value to Helen. When she recovered, I could give it to her and tell her how I had come by it. Then it dawned on me I hadn't seen Tommy since morning.

Chapter Nine

Ada and I fixed spaghetti and salad for lunch, using one of the canned tomato paste sauces. The boys were hungry, but Vicki, Ada and I didn't eat much. And no one felt like talking. Charlie didn't want to come downstairs, so Ada took him up a tray.

Joe Hinkley came back and hosed out the pool, then filled it. When it was full it was very pretty, and the sun shining on it made it sparkle like diamonds.

Vicki said, "I wish I knew how to swim. I'd like to go in."

I knew John and Tony were good swimmers, and the natural thing for them to do would have been to say they would teach her. But they didn't. Instead, John asked, "How about it, Cheryl? Did you bring a suit?"

John and I had often swum together during the time we'd been engaged, so he knew I could swim. I said, "Yes, I did." I glanced around at the rest of them. Ada said, "You couldn't pay me to let myself be seen in a bathing suit."

I said, "Oh, come now; you're not that bad."

She smiled. "I don't much care for fresh water bathing anyway."

John asked, "Tony?"

Tony said, "Sure, I'll go in with you."

The three of us went upstairs to change. I dropped off my blouse and slacks, bra and girdle, and threw them on the bed. I'd put them away when I came up to dress for dinner. Then I slipped on my suit. It was a modified bikini, and I knew I looked well in it. I hoped John would like it. It was more daring than anything I'd ever worn with him.

The rest of the afternoon the three of us swam, floated, raced each other and just played around in the water. It was wonderful. Then we pulled ourselves out and sunned ourselves on towels we'd spread on the lawn that surrounded the pool.

Ada and Vicki had gone upstairs, and a couple of times I thought I saw Vicki watching us from her window, but when I waved she disappeared.

I needn't have worried about my suit. From the look John gave me when I came out on the terrace, I knew he approved. So did Tony, who grinned and whistled.

Later, when I went upstairs to dress for dinner, I was surprised to find Vicki in my room. She had my pink blouse in her hands and was examining the charm bracelet which she'd taken from the pocket. She was unperturbed when I came in. As I was in my bare feet, she hadn't heard me. I said, "What are you doing in my room?"

She shrugged. "Just curious. I noticed you

kept feeling of the pocket in your blouse, and you showed John something you had in it out there in the field. So I was wondering what it was that worried you so much."

I went to her and snatched the bracelet. "Get out of here!" I told her, so angry I could scarcely speak.

She threw the blouse on the bed. "Where did you get Helen's bracelet?" she asked, her eyes narrowing to slits.

I slid the bracelet onto my left wrist. "None of your business!"

"Does Dirk know you have it? Or did he give it to you perhaps?"

"That's none of your business either. Now get out!"

But she just stood there with a sly look on her face. I tried to push her toward the door, but she fought me. "Get out of my room!" I finally screamed at her.

Just then Tony and John came upstairs and heard us. They both ran to the door. "What's the matter?" John asked.

Vicki said, "Nothing," and walked toward the door. But Tony stopped her. Taking her by the shoulders, he held her so she couldn't move and asked, "What are you up to now?" His large brown eyes held no softness as they looked down into her face, and I noticed she avoided meeting them. "Nothing," she said defiantly. "And take your hands off me!"

She tried to wrench herself free of him, but

couldn't. Looking over her head at me, he asked, "Was she bothering you?"

What could I say but, "No, not really."

Without another word he propelled Vicki out of the room, then along the hall into her own room, and shut the door on her.

John looked inquiringly at me. All he had on was a pair of light blue swim trunks; his skin had taken on a nice tan from our hours in the sun in and beside the pool. I held out my left wrist and shook the bracelet so it tinkled. "When I came upstairs she was in here," I told him. "She had my blouse and had taken the bracelet out of the pocket."

"How did she know it was in the pocket?"

"She saw me showing you something when we were in the field, and she was curious and wanted to know what it was."

"Did she get a good look at it?"

"Yes. She recognized it as Helen's."

"Do you want me to keep it until you can give it to Helen?"

I slipped it off my wrist and gave it to him. "Will you, please?"

He took it, stood looking at me thoughtfully for a moment, started to speak, changed his mind. Then he turned away. "I'd better get dressed," he said, and went to his room.

I showered and dressed in a black skirt and ruffled white blouse and buckled a wide black leather belt around my waist. It was the Bonnie and Clyde look.

When I went downstairs Charlie, John and Tony were on the terrace. Dirk hadn't returned from the hospital. John said, "We've just been talking. We thought it would be a good idea to eat out tonight. You girls won't feel like cooking."

I sank down in a wicker chair with my back to the pool. "Good idea. We could walk down to that little restaurant on the green. But I warn you, the woman at the cash register is a gossip, and she's on Harvey's side."

"Why should anyone take sides?" Tony asked. "Is that what they do in country towns?"

"That seems to be what they're doing in this one."

"But why? What's it all about?"

"All I know is that Dirk's cousin wants to buy this house, and Dirk won't sell it."

"But is that any reason for shooting at him and almost killing Helen?"

"It wouldn't seem so. But maybe there's more to it than that. And we don't know that Harvey did do those things."

Charlie was puffing on his pipe. "Maybe we'd all better go back to the city where all that happens is an occasional riot," he said.

Tony laughed. "I'd sort of like to stick around and find out what it is all about."

John's eyes met mine. "The feud between Dirk and his cousin is really none of our business. What worries me is the feud between Vicki and Cheryl."

108

I shook my head at him. "Oh, John, it isn't a feud. Vicki apparently is going through a bad time, and I'm the nearest thing at hand to be the whipping boy for her."

A frown puckered Tony's smooth brow. "What Vicki needs is a good spanking," he said, his jaw squared and his lips tight.

"And who is going to give it to me? You?" Vicki was standing just inside the screen door. She had on white shorts and a dark blue tailored blouse, unbuttoned farther down the front than it should have been.

Without bothering to look at her, Tony said, "I will if you don't behave yourself."

She came out onto the terrace. Her long platinum hair glistened like silver. She looked very cute and desirable, but no one seemed to desire her, least of all Tony or John. She came over to Tony, sat down on his lap and put her arms around his neck. "You don't really mean that," she said, rubbing her cheek against his.

A pulse in his left temple started to throb, and his face flushed. His large brown eyes darkened, and his jaw was clenched. Without a word he took Vicki's arms from around his neck and stood up, dumping her unceremoniously onto the flagstones of the terrace. She cried out and clutched at him, but he eluded her and went into the house, banging the screen door behind him.

John helped her to her feet, and she sank down onto the chair Tony had vacated. Then she covered her face with her hands and began to cry. We just sat there and watched her for a few moments, no one offering any sympathy. Finally Charlie said, "And I came up here for a rest."

Just then Ada came out. "What's the matter with Tony?" she asked. "He came in the back door and went out the front door like he was shot out of a cannon." Then she saw Vicki sitting there crying. "Oh, for heaven sakes!" she said. "Did they have a fight?"

I said, "Just a little misunderstanding."

Ada went to a wicker chair and sat down. "Well," she sighed, "never a dull moment."

Vicki took her hands from her face and sniffled. "I want to go home," she said, stifling a sob.

John lit a cigarette. "I guess we will all be going home soon," he said. "Dirk won't want to go on with the picture after what's happened to Helen."

Ada said, "I wonder how she is. Perhaps we'd better call the hospital."

"I don't think they'd tell us anything," I said. "Dirk will come back as soon as he can. Or he will call us."

It was beginning to get dark, and I knew the men must be getting hungry. But with things the way they were between Vicki and Tony, I didn't think it would be very pleasant to go out to a restaurant. I said to Ada, "The boys suggested we eat out, but we have so much food in the house it seems a shame to spend additional money in a restaurant."

Vicki got up and went into the house, and I wondered if I should follow her. And where had Tony gone?

Ada said, "We could have that steak and frozen vegetables. That wouldn't take long to fix."

Charlie said, "Suits me," and John agreed, "Anything as long as it's food. I wonder if there's an outside grill around anywhere? We could do the steak out here."

"If there's any charcoal," I said.

John got up. "I'll rout around. Maybe there's some in the barn."

I said, "I don't think so. I was in there the day we came up, and I didn't see either charcoal or a grill."

"How about the cellar? There must be one."

I said, "Yes, but how to get into the cellar is another matter. There is a bulkhead near the side door to the kitchen, but there must be a way to go down from inside the house."

Ada said, "Of course there must be." So we all went into the house and began opening doors. John found the cellar door in the kitchen pantry. "Here it is," he said. "Strange place to have it." He snapped on a light at the head of the stairs and went down. He was gone quite awhile, and Ada and I began assembling things for dinner. The steak was frozen, but it would thaw, and there were a couple of boxes of frozen French fries and two of string beans. And there was salad makings.

I took everything out of the refrigerator and put the things on the drain board beside the sink. Then I stood there, feeling as frozen as the vegetables and the steak. Someone was crying, the kind of crying I had heard in the night. We looked at each other. "Vicki?" Ada asked.

I said, "I don't think so."

"Where is it coming from?"

"I can't tell."

Then suddenly it stopped, and a cold chill went up my back. I said, "I wonder what is keeping John so long."

"Maybe we'd better call him."

I went into the pantry and looked down into the dimly lit cellar. John was standing beside an old trunk. On top of it was a portable record player. I called, "Can you find anything?"

He looked up at me. "No grill or charcoal, but come down and look at this." He nodded to the record player.

I went down and stood beside him. He started the record that was on the machine, and the crying commenced.

I grabbed his arm. "Stop it!" I cried. "Oh, stop it!" So he clicked it off.

"What's the matter?" he asked.

"I don't know, but — Oh, let's go upstairs!" I turned and ran up to the pantry, and John followed me.

When we were back in the kitchen, he asked, "What are you so upset about?"

Ada was standing at the sink, her face white, her eyes wide with fright. "What is it?" she asked in a shaky voice.

John said, "A record. It's just a record of someone crying; maybe a sound effect record Dirk made sometime."

Ada and I looked at each other, and finally I was able to ask, "But who turns it on in the middle of the night? Surely not Dirk."

John looked bewildered. "What do you mean?" he asked.

Ada said, "Haven't you heard it? The crying in the night?"

"Well, yes. But I thought it was one of you girls. Girls are always crying."

I smiled. "No we aren't either. Not like that."

Ada said, "I wonder if Dirk knows about it. The record player, I mean."

I shook my head. "I doubt it. He hasn't been up here since his aunt's funeral last summer."

John rammed his hands into the pockets of his slacks and walked over to the side door. For a moment he stood looking out at the barn. "Queer business," he said. "I think I'll go out and have a look at that bulkhead." He went out but was back in a few moments. "The cellar door to that wasn't locked. I've locked it."

Ada said, "Maybe we should call the police."

John said, "What good would that do?"

"They could take fingerprints."

John shook his head. "They'd be sure to find all kinds of fingerprints. Don't forget this is a very old house."

"But if they found Harvey's?"

"Wouldn't prove a thing. He's probably been in and out and all around this house for years. His fingerprints must be all over the place."

Ada sighed. "Yes, I suppose so." Then she became practical again. "Well, I take it you didn't find an outside grill or any charcoal?"

John said, "No."

"Well then, I'd better light the broiler in the stove."

Neither Ada nor I had seen anything of Vicki since she'd slammed into the house after the fracas with Tony, so it came as a surprise to Ada, when she went out to the terrace to tell Charlie dinner was ready, to find her on Charlie's lap and him kissing her.

John had disappeared after we'd come up from the cellar, and I looked out on the terrace to see if he was there. He wasn't, but I was just in time to see Ada pull Vicki off Charlie's lap and give her a good shaking. "You let my Charlie alone," Ada cried, "or I'll yank some of that bleached blonde hair right out of your silly head!"

Vicki backed away from her, momentarily frightened. Then she laughed. "Oh, don't worry; I don't want him. I just felt sorry for him. He doesn't have much fun with *you*."

Ada took a step toward her, her hand raised to slap her face, but I rushed out and stepped between them. "Please!" I cried. "Stop! What's the matter with everybody anyway?"

Charlie got to his feet; he seemed to be standing taller and straighter than usual. He had lipstick on his cheek and some on his lips. "I'm sorry, Ada," he said, trying to put an arm around her. "Vicki's just a child. It didn't mean anything."

Ada pushed him away and went into the house and upstairs to her room. We could hear the door slam way down there on the terrace.

For a moment I stood there, not knowing what to do. Then I remembered the steak on the platter and the vegetables on the dining table. Fortunately they were in covered serving dishes, so they would keep warm for a while. "Anybody know where John is?" I asked.

Charlie said, "No, I haven't seen him for a while."

"I wonder if he is upstairs." I went into the hall and called, "John! Where are you?"

He came out of the living room. He had a grin on his face. "Having more troubles?" he asked.

"Did you see that?" I nodded toward the terrace.

"Yes. If anybody around here gets murdered, there will be so many suspects the police won't know where to begin."

I tried to smile but couldn't manage it. I

asked, "Has Tony turned up?"

John said, "Haven't seen him."

I sighed. "Well, dinner is ready, if anyone has any appetite. It's all on the table. If you'll get Vicki and Charlie in, I'll go up and see if I can pacify Ada." But when I knocked on her door she said, "Go away!" She sounded as if she were crying.

I called, "It's me, Ada. Come on down and have your dinner."

"I don't want any."

"Shall I bring you up a tray?"

"No, thank you."

I gave up and went downstairs. Vicki, Charlie and John were at the dining table, and John was carving the steak. I sat down beside him and served the vegetables onto each plate as he passed it to me with a piece of steak on it. Charlie asked, "Is Ada coming down?" The lipstick was still smeared on his face, and he looked ridiculous.

I said, "No."

"Should I go up and get her?"

"I wouldn't, if I were you."

"Oh dear!" He sighed. "Now I'm going to be in for it."

Vicki snickered. John gave her a look of complete disapproval, but she just grinned impishly and began to eat.

We were nearly through and ready for our coffee when Dirk came in. He looked unutterably tired. Seeing us in the dining room, he came in and sank down on a chair.

I asked, "How did you get back?"

"Doctor Brooks brought me."

"Had any dinner?"

"No."

So John and I fixed a plate for him, and he tried to eat but couldn't. I asked, "How is Helen?"

"Not too good. She has a concussion, and they gave her a transfusion. She's under sedation now."

John asked, "Did she say anything?"

"No. She doesn't seem to remember much."

I asked, "Is she under guard?"

"What do you mean?"

"If she ever remembers what happened to her, she could get somebody into trouble."

A hopeless look came over his face, and he pushed his plate away, leaning an elbow on the table and resting his head on his hand. "I never thought of that. If she remembers, whoever it was who attacked her may try to keep her from telling."

"It's logical."

He sighed heavily. "I hate to stir up a fuss at the hospital."

"Rather that than have someone get to Helen while she's asleep."

He didn't say anything for a long time; just sat there with his eyes closed. Then he seemed to jerk himself into action. His eyes opened, and he got up from his chair. "I'll call Doctor

117

Brooks and explain it to him. Maybe he can arrange to have a nurse with her at all times." He went into the living room and picked up the phone, and I began gathering up the soiled dishes. John got up and took his and Charlie's. "I'll help you with these," he said. "You seem to be doing all the work."

I gave him a grateful smile, and Vicki said, "Oh brother!"

Over his shoulder John told her to "Shut up!"

Out in the kitchen, he said to me, "I wonder where Tony went."

"I don't know. Maybe he's up in his room."

"He isn't. I looked."

"Out in the barn?"

"No. I looked there too."

"I don't think there's any place he can get a drink."

"He's not much of a drinker. But maybe he's gone down to that restaurant on the green for his dinner, to get away from the mess here."

I said, "Maybe. As soon as we have our coffee, let's go down and see." I put the glass percolator, cups, saucers, cream and sugar on a tray, and John took it into the dining room.

Dirk had finished his phone call to the doctor and was back at the table. He said, "Doctor Brooks is taking care of it."

We all drank our coffee without talking until Dirk suddenly asked, "Where are Ada and Tony?"

For a moment no one answered; then John said, "That's kind of a long story."

Dirk looked startled. "Oh? What?"

I said, "Nothing serious. Just a couple of mis- understandings."

Dirk swallowed the rest of his coffee and set the cup down on the saucer with a bang. "What next?" he asked wearily.

I reached over and refilled his cup. "Would you like us all to go home? I guess you won't want to go on with the picture now, will you?"

He looked down into his coffee cup. "I don't know," he said. "I hate to give up now."

I said, "Maybe we could do it some other time."

He shook his head. "No. If we quit now, we'll never all be able to get up here together again."

No one said anything, and he stirred his coffee thoughtfully. Then he looked up at us; at John, Charlie, Vicki and me. "If you can stick it out, I can," he said, a defiant look in his eyes.

I knew his defiance wasn't for us but for fate, that had gotten things into such a mess. I felt so sorry for him I could have hugged him, but I knew better than to try. Kissing Tony because I felt sorry for him had precipitated one of our upsets. I didn't want to cause another. So I said, "I'll stay if the rest will."

"You can count on me," John said.

"Me too — if Ada will stay," Charlie said.

Dirk looked at Vicki. "And you?"

119

She shrugged. "Why not?" she said, not too enthusiastically.

Dirk began to perk up. He drank his second cup of coffee quickly, then said, "Okay. Why don't we run through the first scene of the second act up in my room where we have all the props?"

I said, "Shall we leave the dishes, or shall I do them first?"

"Oh, leave them. I'll help you with them later."

As it happened, we didn't need either Ada or Tony for that particular scene. It was between John and Vicki and me. But I was uneasy about Tony's absence. I would have spoken to Dirk about it, but he had enough on his mind.

We didn't know our lines well enough to rehearse without our scripts, and they had all been left out on the terrace. Dirk got them and said, "Come on. We'll just go through it once to get the feel of the furniture and the groupings."

Charlie, not being needed, suggested, "I think I'll chance going up to Ada." That gave me the opening I'd been waiting for. I said, "Before you go, would you mind taking a walk over to that restaurant on the green and seeing if Tony is there?"

Dirk asked, "Why would Tony be over there?"

John answered for me. "We're not sure he is, but he went out several hours ago, and there isn't any other place he could go, is there?"

Dirk ran his hand through his hair. "But there is plenty of food here in the house."

I asked, "Could he get a drink over there?"

"Only beer. And we have that in the refrigerator."

Dirk turned to Vicki. "Did you and he have a fight?"

She tossed her long platinum hair over her shoulder. "Of course not. I never fight with my men."

Dirk didn't bother to answer that. He just said, "Well, let's go upstairs."

Chapter Ten

As we were going up the stairs, Charlie went out the front door. By then it was almost dark, and Dirk snapped on the hall lights.

We'd just reached the upper hall when Ada's door opened. Her eyes were red-rimmed, her face blotchy and her hair disheveled. "Where is Charlie going?" she demanded. "I just saw him going down the road."

John said, "Only over to the restaurant on the green to look for Tony."

She heaved a big sigh and began smoothing down her hair. "Darn it!" she said. "Now I'll have to go after him."

Dirk gave me a glance that I knew meant, "Help me," so I said to Ada, "You can't go looking like that. You'll have to wash your face in cold water and put on fresh makeup."

She thought that over for a moment, then turned back into her room. "I guess you're right," she said. "I probably look a mess."

Dirk motioned the rest of us into his room and snapped on the lights. "Now what I want for the present is for you to take your places so you'll get accustomed to where you are supposed to be during each of your lines."

Inadvertently I glanced at the rocking chair.

It wasn't moving, but it was in the shadows. However, the scene was laid in the early morning, so when it was filmed it would be bright daylight.

As the scene panned in, Allister and Deborah were just getting out of bed, one on one side and the other on the opposite side. The bed was placed against the wall at the end of the room, so there was ample space to get in and out on either side.

As they got up they slipped their feet into slippers that were on the floor where they would be convenient and then each reached for a robe. Allister's was on a chair near his side of the bed, and Deborah's was hanging on the bedpost at the foot of the bed on her side. They both yawned but did not speak. They were still angry at each other because of the previous evening.

Allister began to assemble his clothes, then ambled toward the bathroom, yawning and scratching his tousled head. Deborah went to her dressing table and began to examine her face, sighed, got up and wandered around assembling her clothing; fresh underwear from a drawer in the highboy, stockings, bra, girdle, then slacks and a tailored blouse.

Water from the shower could be heard; then Allister began to sing, "Oh, what a beautiful morning."

Deborah put a hand to her forehead and said, "Ugh! Beautiful! Ha! What's beautiful about it?" She went to the phone on the table on Allister's side of the bed, dialed a number. When she got it she said, "Dad, Deborah."

Then, "No! *Nothing* is all right. And I've had enough. I've got a wonderful idea. Why don't you and I take that trip around the world we used to talk about?" I looked at Dirk. "We need Charlie here. His voice is supposed to be heard on the phone."

Dirk said, "That's right. Well, I'll do his part." Imitating the sound of a voice coming over the phone, he said, "But you can't do that. You can't leave Allister now."

Deborah said, "What's to stop me?"

Voice on phone: "If you do you're a little fool. He needs you more than ever now."

Deborah: "He never needed me. He just needs himself and whatever cute little number is around at the moment. This time it's Rosemary."

Just then there was a knock on the door; then it opened and Rosemary came into the room, fresh and bright in shorts and a very revealing turtle-necked sweater. "Did I hear my name?" she asked sweetly.

Deborah said a quick, "Goodbye, Dad; I'll call you later," replaced the receiver then turned to Rosemary. "How did you get in?"

"Your maid let me in." She strolled over to the dressing table and smoothed her hair. "As a matter of fact, I came for a swim."

"Well, you can just go. We aren't swimming this morning."

The bathroom door opened and Allister came into the room, freshly shaven, his hair slicked down, wearing gray slacks and a blue plaid sports shirt. He saw Rosemary, and his face brightened. "Well, good morning. What gets you out so early?"

She ran to him and grabbed his arms. "You! Oh, Allister, I didn't sleep a wink all night." She tried to kiss him, but he held her so she couldn't.

Deborah said, "Pardon me," and went into the bathroom with her clothing. She pushed the door to but didn't shut it.

Dirk said to John, "Now here is where you tell her to go over and sit in the rocker and wait until Deborah comes out of the bathroom, and then you'll all go down to breakfast."

I was standing in the bathroom with the door almost closed, letting the shower run, when I heard Vicki scream. She screamed so loudly I could hear it above the noise of the shower. I knew the scream wasn't in the script, so I opened the door to see what the matter was.

Vicki was standing looking at the rocking chair, her eyes wide, her face white. She was pointing to the chair, and she looked frightened to death. "It pushed me!" she cried. "Somebody pushed me!"

Dirk said, "Nonsense. There is no one there to push you. You can see for yourself. Now then, try it again. Allister says to you, 'Go over there and sit down until Deborah comes out of the bathroom, and then we'll all go down to breakfast.' And you go over and sit in the rocking chair and begin to rock impatiently."

Vicki whirled on him. "No! No! I won't do it! I tell you, just as I was sitting down in the chair someone pushed me. I could feel two hands on my back, and they gave me a push! You saw how I almost fell down!"

Dirk and I exchanged glances, and John just stood there. He was chewing on one side of his lower lip, and I could tell he'd had about enough of the Manor House in Mount Sharon, Massachusetts. I said, "Don't be ridiculous, Vicki. You can see yourself there is nothing there."

She stared at the chair and shook her head. "Nothing we can *see*," she said, "but something I could *feel!*" The chair was rocking slowly. She backed away from it, and John put his arms around her. "Look!" she cried. "It's rocking!"

Dirk said, "That's because you started it when you went to sit in it."

She was trembling now. "But I never even touched it," she said in an awed voice. "Before I could sit down on it, I was pushed away."

Dirk threw his script down on the bed. "I give up!" he said. "Take a break. That's all for tonight."

I took my script into my room and left it on the bureau, and Dirk, John and Vicki went downstairs.

I went into the bathroom for a moment, and

when I followed them downstairs I heard the piano. I knew it was John playing. I'd always enjoyed the way he had of improvising. I could hear Dirk cleaning up the dinner dishes and knew I should go help him, but I couldn't resist first going into the living room and listening to John for a few minutes. I hurried into the living room, then stopped and caught my breath. John was at the piano, yes, but standing behind him with her arms around his neck and her cheek against his head was Vicki. Instantly I had a strong urge to go over and pull her away from John, the way Ada had pulled her away from Charlie. But I realized that would be foolish. I didn't have a claim to John any more, and if he didn't want her hugging him like that he could have stopped her. Neither of them saw me, and I backed out of the room and ran through the dining room to the kitchen, almost bumping into Dirk as he was taking a tray of soiled dishes to the sink. I said, "Oh, I'm sorry."

He put the tray down and gave me a surprised look. "*Now* what's the matter?" he asked.

"Oh, nothing. I was coming to help you."

"Looking as if you'd seen a ghost? Don't tell me Aunt Suzy pushed *you* too."

I shook my head. "No, nothing like that. Just — oh, nothing." I went to the sink and began scraping and rinsing the dishes so Dirk could put them into the dishwasher.

He stood and watched me for a few minutes,

then said, "Tell me what happened this afternoon while I was over at the hospital."

"Oh, it was really nothing."

"It must have been something to have caused Ada to shut herself up in her room and cry, and Tony to disappear and not come back for dinner. Was it Vicki?"

"Well, yes. But everybody makes so much of so little."

He stopped loading the dishwasher and looked at my flushed face. I knew it must be flushed because it felt so warm. He said, "And *now* don't you think maybe *you* are making too much of something rather small?"

"I don't know what you mean."

"Don't you?"

"No."

"Isn't that John playing the piano?"

"Yes."

"Is he alone?"

"No."

"Then there is only one person who could be with him."

I blinked back the tears that suddenly flooded my eyes. Then between clenched teeth I said, "She can *have* him! *I* don't want him!"

Dirk began stacking the dishes in the dishwasher again. "That's right; you don't," he said. "You didn't even want to come up here because he was coming."

I didn't say anything. What was the use? I knew Dirk had seen the way John and I had been drawing closer and closer together ever since we'd arrived.

After a moment Dirk said, "I wonder how Helen is. Is it too late to call the hospital?"

"It's after ten. If she's still under sedation, there won't be anything they can tell you."

"No, I suppose not."

We'd finished putting the dishes into the washer when I remembered the record player in the cellar. I asked, "Have you got a record player down in the cellar?"

He looked at me in surprise. "No. And I never heard of Aunt Suzy having one. Why?"

"I was just wondering. Have you ever made or bought any sound effect records?"

"No. Why do you ask?"

"You don't know of a record of a woman crying?"

He stared at me. "No. What on earth are you talking about?"

I leaned back against the sink. "Since we've been up here, you haven't heard a woman crying in the middle of the night?"

"Well, yes, I have. But I thought it was one of you girls."

"That's what we all thought. But it wasn't. It's a record on a player down in the cellar."

He stared at me. "You're kidding."

"Go see for yourself."

Without another word he went into the pantry and down to the cellar. In a moment the sound of the crying commenced. Then it stopped, and Dirk came upstairs. "Well, I'll be darned!" he said. "I wonder how that got there?"

"I thought you would know."

"Me? Why?"

I shrugged. "It's your house."

He ran his hand through his hair. "Yes, so it is," he said. "But who starts it playing in the middle of the night?"

"We thought maybe you did."

His face tensed. "Why on earth would I do that?"

"To frighten us, make us think there is a ghost in the house."

He smiled a little at that. "Well, there is. But she doesn't cry." He thought a moment; then, "Someone wants to scare us away. And whoever it is has access to the house."

"Would Harvey have a key?"

He walked over to the side door and stared out into the darkness. "He easily could have."

"And would he stoop to such a childish trick?"

With his back to me, Dirk said, "Oh, yes. That's just the silly kind of thing he would think of."

"Why don't you break the record and see if we hear the crying tonight?"

He whirled around. "Good idea." He returned to the cellar and brought up the record. Then he put it on the floor and stepped on it. It was an old 78, and it broke easily. "There," he said. He got a broom and dustpan and swept up the pieces and threw them into the garbage can.

The piano playing had stopped, but Vicki and John were still in the living room. At least they hadn't joined us out in the kitchen, and I could see out of the window that they weren't on the terrace.

We had all the dinner dishes in the washer, and Dirk turned it on. "Come on; let's get out of here," he said. "It will turn off automatically. Let's go see what Vicki and John are doing."

I followed him into the hall, but I just couldn't go into the living room. I said, "I think I'll go up to bed."

But Dirk took hold of my arm. "No, don't do that. You're a good actress — remember? And anything you see in the living room isn't going to affect you. Or if it does, you're not going to show it."

I held back for a moment, but Dirk insisted, and together we went into the living room.

John was sitting in one of the easy chairs, reading a book. He looked up when we came in. Dirk asked. "Where's Vicki?"

John closed the book and took out a cigarette. "She went up to bed."

Dirk and I sat down near John, and the two men lit cigarettes. I said, "Won't you play some more? It sounded good."

John got up and went to the piano. "Anything to please a lady," he said, and began to play one of the current hit tunes. I wanted desperately to go over and stand behind him and put my arms around his neck the way Vicki had, but of course I couldn't and wouldn't.

Dirk finished his cigarette. "I think I'll go to bed," he said.

John stopped playing. I didn't want to be left alone with him, so I said, "I think I will too. Thanks, John. I enjoyed it."

He said, "My pleasure," and lit another cigarette. "I'll wait up for Tony," he added.

Dirk said, "I can't imagine where he is. Even if he'd gone down to that restaurant on the green, it closes at nine, and it's after ten now."

"And Ada and Charlie are still out," I reminded him.

Just then the front door opened and Ada came in. She looked as if she'd been crying again. "I've been sitting on the front steps," she said. "I went down to that restaurant, but it was closed."

"Then you didn't find either Charlie or Tony?"

"No."

"That's strange," Dirk said. "They don't have a car to go anywhere. They didn't take my station wagon or Cheryl's car, did they?"

"No. They are both out in the driveway by the barn. Besides, you didn't leave the keys in them, did you?"

Dirk and I both said, "No."

"Maybe they got acquainted with someone in

the restaurant and went home with him," John suggested.

"Unh, unh," Dirk said. "This is New England. People don't get acquainted with strangers so quickly."

"Maybe they met Harvey there," I suggested.

Dirk looked upset by that idea. "That could have happened," he said. "Annie Bradley is a friend of Emma's. I guess they go there quite often."

Ada sighed. "If they get Charlie started drinking again, I'll never forgive them."

"Is Harvey a drinker?" I asked Dirk.

"Not that I know of. He's superintendent of the Sunday school and vice president of the bank. He couldn't very well keep those jobs if he drank."

"No, I suppose not."

"Maybe he just invited Tony and Charlie home for coffee after the restaurant closed."

"That could be. He might have wanted to pump them."

"About what?"

"Me, of course."

Ada said, "Well, I might as well go up to bed."

"Me too," I said.

John said, "Good night. If they don't come back pretty soon, I'll go up too."

Dirk said, "If you do, lock the doors and windows. When they come home, I'll go down and let them in."

So Ada, Dirk and I went upstairs. In the upper hall we exchanged good nights, and as I went to my room I noticed Vicki's door was closed and there was no light showing beneath it. Her bathroom door was also closed.

It didn't take me long to get into bed, but I couldn't go to sleep. I kept listening for Tony and Charlie to come in. For a while John played the piano softly, and I lay in my bed remembering the times he used to play for me when we were going together. I play a little myself and have a small spinet in my studio apartment.

After a while the playing stopped, and I could hear John going around the first floor shutting and locking doors and windows. Then he came upstairs and went into his room.

I must have fallen asleep before Tony and Charlie came back, because I didn't hear them. And there was no sound of a woman crying, as on the previous nights. The first thing I knew it was daylight. I stretched and yawned and glanced at the clock. It was six-thirty. I sat up, swung my legs over the side of the bed and put my feet into my slippers; then I stood up and wandered over to one of the windows. The air was clear and fresh, and the sun was shining on the water at the far end of the pool, making it sparkle like diamonds. But near the terrace, where the sun didn't reach this early in the morning, the pool was darker and — I took a second look — there was something floating in the dark water. A body? The body of a girl, a girl with long platinum hair. And the hair was spread out around her head like a fan, floating on top of the water.

I stifled a scream and clapped my hands to my mouth. Then I cried, "Vicki!" I ran into the bathroom and opened the door to her room. It wasn't locked, and the room was empty. The bed had been slept in but was empty now. I looked around. The door to the hall was open. I ran out into the hall. All the other doors were closed; Dirk's and the one to Tony's and John's room; also the one to Ada's and Charlie's room.

I ran to Dirk's door and began to knock on it, gently at first, then harder. After a few moments he called, "Yes? Who is it?"

I called, "It's me, Cheryl. Come quick. Vicki's in the pool!"

I heard his feet land on the floor with a thud, then pound across the floor, and the door opened. "What?" he asked, stifling a yawn. His hair was tousled, and he looked like a small boy.

"Vicki!" I gasped. "In the pool! Floating!"

Dirk yawned openly. "So? She probably wanted to take an early swim."

"But she can't swim!" I cried. "And she's floating face down!"

The door to John's and Tony's room opened, and John asked, "What's the matter?"

"Vicki!" I gasped. "In the pool! Dead!"

"Oh, good God!" John cried, and he and Dirk raced downstairs, with me after them.

The three of us practically tumbled out onto the terrace and down to the pool. Vicki was still there, floating face down, her long platinum hair spreading out from her head.

Dirk and John both jumped into the pool and swam over to her, towing her to the end where there was a ladder. Together they lifted her body out of the water onto the lawn sur-rounding the pool. She was wearing a mini-nightdress that scarcely covered her cold white body.

I knelt beside her and pulled it down as best I could. The boys knelt on the other side and turned her over. Her eyes were open, and she looked horrible. I covered my face with my hands and began to shiver. John said, "Do you think there's any use giving her artificial respi-ration?"

Dirk put his ear to her chest, then raised his head. "No. It's too late," he said, and his broad shoulders sagged. Then he pointed to her neck. There were bruises on it. "She must have scraped her neck on the edge of the pool as she fell in," he said.

I managed to pull myself together and get to my feet. "Had I better call Doctor Brooks?" I asked.

Dirk said, "I'll call him — and the police." He got to his feet and went into the kitchen to phone.

John rose and stood looking down at what used to be Vicki. I said, "I'm sorry — if you liked her."

John looked at me as if he hadn't heard me correctly. "Liked her?" he repeated. "Poor kid — nobody *liked* her. But who *hated* her enough to kill her?"

"Tony — maybe?" I almost whispered it, shocked that I should even have the thought.

"Of course not!" John snapped. "What a thing to say!" He looked angry now, and I shuddered. But I managed to ask, "Did he come back last night?"

John nodded. "Yes. About midnight."

"Did he say where they were?"

"Over at Harvey's, just as we thought."

"Had they been drinking?"

"Just beer, before they left the restaurant. Charlie was a little crocked, but Tony was all right."

Dirk returned from making his phone calls. "Doctor Brooks will be right over, and so will the police," he said. "You'd better go up and get dressed, Cheryl." It wasn't until then that I realized I didn't have anything over my pale pink mini-nightdress. I turned and ran into the house and up the stairs.

Ada's and Charlie's door was still closed, but John had left his open, and Tony was sitting on the side of the bed, scratching his tousled head and yawning. "Hi," he said. "What's all the commotion?"

I stopped at the door just long enough to say, "Vicki! In the pool! Dead!" Then a sob choked me and I ran to my room, slamming the door.

Chapter Eleven

I dressed as quickly as I could, all the time wondering who could have killed Vicki. Surely Ada wouldn't have, just because Charlie had kissed her. Nor would John. She annoyed him, but not enough for him to kill her. And Dirk was too upset about Helen to bother with her. Besides, he had no reason to dislike her. He seemed completely neutral as far as she was concerned.

Of all of us, Tony had the strongest motive, and if the police found out he'd once been Vicki's husband they would think that sufficient reason to be suspicious of him.

And what about me? If it came out that Vicki and I had been having altercations, I would naturally come under suspicion. I was sure Harvey would be only too glad to tell how he'd seen me slap Vicki that first night. And if John and Tony told them about our fight over Helen's bracelet, that would deepen their suspicions. I knew the boys wouldn't mention it on their own, but the police have clever ways of getting people to talk.

I heard cars arriving and men's voices. I went to the window and looked out. Doctor Brooks was kneeling beside Vicki, and there were two state policemen asking Dirk and John questions. Tony was there also, down on his knees beside Vicki. He was talking to the doctor and seemed very upset. I remembered his telling me that he still loved Vicki. And now she was dead. Surely it must be a terrible blow to him. But if he had killed her himself — ?

I wondered if I should go down and join them. It was only a matter of time before the police would be questioning all of us. But first there would be the coroner and the homicide squad, if they had such things in small country villages. If not there would be a sheriff, and newspaper reporters and photographers from surrounding towns. News of this kind spread quickly. It was going to be horrible. And what of Helen, lying in the hospital, with Dirk unable to get over to see her because of this latest tragedy?

I decided I'd better go and awaken Ada and Charlie and tell them what had happened. They would want to be up and dressed before the police came looking for them.

I went over and knocked on their door. In a moment Ada called, "Yes?"

"It's me. Cheryl. Can I talk to you?"

She opened the door. She was dressed in a cotton print shirtwaist dress, and she looked as if she hadn't slept much. Charlie was still in bed, but my knock on the door and Ada's and my voices had awakened him. Ada asked, "Are we late for breakfast?"

I said, "No. There probably won't be any breakfast. We've had — there's been another tragedy."

Ada's eyes widened. "Oh? What?"

"Vicki. When I got up a little while ago, I looked out my window and saw Vicki in the pool. She was floating face down, and she was dead!"

"What?" Charlie bounced out of bed.

I said, "Vicki. She's dead." I noticed the bottom of his pajama legs were wet, and there was a drying puddle of water on the floor where he was standing.

He sank down on the side of the bed and stared at me. "Was it an accident?" he asked.

"We don't know. She didn't know how to swim, and she was in her nightdress. She could have gone down for some air and slipped." The idea had just occurred to me, and I held onto it, glad to have something to explain Vicki's demise other than murder. "She probably thought everybody would still be asleep, so she hadn't bothered to put on a robe or anything."

Ada stood looking at me, her hand still on the knob of the door. "There are probably plenty of people who would have enjoyed murdering her," she said, her face tense, her eyes cold and with a glint in them.

From halfway up the stairs a policeman asked, "Who, for instance?" Dirk was behind him.

Ada said an explosive, "Oh!" and closed the

door. It almost banged into my nose. I stepped back and turned to the policeman and Dirk, who by then had reached the top of the stairs. I said, "Ada and Charlie are just getting up."

The policeman seemed undisturbed by Ada's rudeness.

Dirk said, "Cheryl, this is Lieutenant Vance. Lieutenant, Miss Cheryl Daniels."

I said, "How do you do," and the lieutenant said, "Miss Daniels."

Dirk stated "The lieutenant wants to have a look at Vicki's room. Will you show him? I want to get dressed."

I said, "Of course. This way, please." I led him through the hall to Vicki's room and watched him as he looked around, seeing the mussed bed, the clothes she'd worn yesterday thrown over a chair, her negligee laying at the foot of the bed. Her slippers weren't anywhere in sight. She must have had them on when she went downstairs. She had probably lost them in the pool, because she hadn't had them on when John and Dirk had pulled her out.

The lieutenant began opening bureau drawers. He looked in the closet, into her suitcase. He said, "Tell me what you know about this girl."

"I don't really know very much. I didn't know her very well."

"Has she any relatives?"

"I don't know. As long as I've known her, she's been on her own in a one-room apartment in the Village. She's an actress. She's been in several road shows, done off Broadway, showcase things — nothing very big."

"Is she married?"

"Not that I know of." Why should I be the one to tell him?

"Any enemies?"

I hesitated. "Not as far as I know."

"Many friends?"

"I really don't know."

"Do people like her?"

I didn't answer that. No one wants to speak ill of the dead.

When I didn't answer, Lieutenant Vance turned and looked at me. "Did *you* like her?"

I met his eyes, which were brown, head on. "Not particularly," I admitted honestly.

"What about the men here? Was she having an affair with any of them?"

"No. *That* I am sure of."

He raised an eyebrow. "Would you have been jealous if she had been?"

I could see where he was leading, so I said a quick, "No. Not at all."

Vicki's purse was laying on top of the bureau. He picked it up and began going through it. There were the usual things that are in every girl's purse; a compact, lipstick, eyebrow stuff, tissues, change, a few bills, keys. There were also the usual credit and identification cards. He read them and replaced them one by one, until he came to the last one. This he read

143

twice. Then he handed it to me. "What do you make of this?" he asked.

I took the card and read it. It was a charge plate of a New York department store, and it was made out in the name of Mrs. Tony Maretti.

My heart gave a jump, and my hand began to shake. I gave the card back to the lieutenant. "I don't know," I said, and my voice sounded queer, "unless she borrowed it from somebody."

"Isn't that the name of one of the men staying here? I was introduced to a Tony Maretti down on the terrace."

I didn't know what to say and was glad that just at that moment Dirk came out of his room, fully dressed in brown slacks and a white sport shirt. He had also shaved. He came over to Vicki's room and asked, "Find anything?"

The lieutenant said, "Nothing but this," and gave him the credit card.

Dirk read it and then looked at me. "Do you know anything about this?" he asked.

I deliberately lied and said, "No, I don't."

The lieutenant put the card into a pocket. "Well, let's go downstairs."

As we passed the closed door to Ada's and Charlie's room, he asked, "Will they be dressed soon? I'd like to talk to them."

I said, "I guess so," and knocked at the door, calling, "Hurry up, folks. You're wanted downstairs." Then I remembered that the lower part of Charlie's pajama pants legs had been wet and wondered if Lieutenant Vance had noticed it.

By the time we got down to the terrace, the coroner had arrived and a photographer was taking pictures.

Tony was standing at the end of the pool, staring down into it. Lieutenant Vance went over to him, said a few words and then showed him the credit card. Tony looked at it, nodded and then gave it back to the lieutenant.

I felt a little sigh of relief escape me, I was so glad that Tony wasn't going to deny his marriage to Vicki. The lieutenant said a few more words to him, then left him standing there at the end of the pool and joined the group around the body of Vicki.

I couldn't resist going over to Tony. I said, "I'm sorry, Tony. Is there anything I can do?"

He shook his head. Then, pointing down at the water, he said, "Look, there at the bottom. They look like her slippers."

I said, "Probably. Later I'll put on my bathing suit and get them for you."

For answer he made a quick dive, swam to the bottom of the pool and came up with the slippers.

When the people over by Vicki heard the splash, they all turned, and Lieutenant Vance hurried over, but by then Tony had surfaced. He had the soaked and sodden slippers in his hand. Without a word he handed them to Lieutenant Vance, then said, "If you'll excuse me, I'll go up and get dressed." His black hair was plastered to his head, his pajama trousers clung to his legs and thighs, and it was impossible to tell whether the moisture in his large dark eyes was chlorinated water from the pool or tears.

Chapter Twelve

Somehow we all got through the rest of the morning. Of course there was the questioning of the police, and unspoken accusations flew back and forth between us. Tony honestly and straightforwardly admitted to having been married to Vicki. He said that as far as he knew, she didn't have any relatives. She'd grown up in an orphanage because her parents had died when she was very young. He said, "Yes, we were divorced, but under the circumstances I shall of course see that she is buried as Mrs. Tony Maretti."

Charlie and Ada were very nervous, and Ada was snappy with Charlie. Dirk was upset about the whole thing, and John stuck close to Tony and did what little he could to make things easy for him.

After the police, the coroner, the photographer, the doctor and an ambulance with Vicki's body had left, I managed to make some coffee and cook bacon and eggs and make a pile of toast. No one felt like eating, but we all tried, and I had to make a second pot of coffee.

Toward the end of the meal Tony asked, "Will there be an autopsy?"

Dirk said, "I suppose so."

"But there really isn't any reason for one. She definitely drowned."

Dirk gulped coffee. "It was an accident, of course. She must have slipped into the pool. It's slippery around the edge, and she couldn't swim."

Tony said, "Yes." His face was white beneath his tan, and there was such a sad look in his big brown eyes that it was heartbreaking.

To change the subject I asked Dirk, "Have you called the hospital about Helen?"

"Oh, my gosh!" he cried, jumped up from the table and went into the living room to phone.

While he was gone no one had anything to say. He returned in a few minutes. "I have to go right over to the hospital," he said. "Helen's awake and has been asking for me."

"Would you like me to drive you over in my car?" I asked him.

"Would you mind?"

"Of course not. I'll get my keys." I jumped up from the table and ran upstairs.

When we went into the hospital, I said, "I'll wait in the reception room."

Dirk said, "All right. I probably won't be long."

But at the door to the reception room we were met by Harvey. He had been standing at a window and had seen us come in. "Dirk!" he said, grabbing hold of his arm. "I've got to talk to you. I've tried and tried to see Helen, but they won't let me." His face was flushed, and he seemed very tense.

Dirk pulled his arm away. "How did you know Helen was here?" he asked.

Harvey shrugged. "Everybody knows everything in a small town. But you must listen to me. Your life is in danger. And so is Helen's."

Dirk looked at him searchingly. He wasn't quite as tall as Harvey, although he carried himself so well he gave the impression of being a tall man. He said, "So it would seem. I didn't realize you wanted the house that badly."

Fortunately, the reception room was empty, so there was no one around to hear the conversation. Harvey still had his arm in a sling. He felt of it gently and winced when his fingers touched a certain spot. "It's not me," he said, dropping his voice to a confidential tone. "It's a syndicate." He shifted his weight from one foot to another. "You see, they want the house for a private gambling place, and they've offered a fantastic price for it. And — well, I thought I was going to inherit the house, so I told them I'd sell it to them."

Dirk watched his cousin's face, his own tight and grim. "And now they are pushing you," he said.

Harvey almost smiled. "Yes — yes, that's it. I knew you'd understand if I explained the situation to you. You see they gave me ten thousand on account and — well, you know how it is —"

"Oh yes, I understand perfectly," Dirk said. "And if you're in a bind, I'm sorry. But I'm still not going to sell you the house."

Harvey grabbed Dirk's shoulder and shook it. "But you've *got* to!" he cried angrily. He was breathing heavily, and his face was getting even redder. "If you don't, they'll kill you. And me. And Helen."

Dirk removed Harvey's hand from his shoulder. "That still wouldn't get them the house," he said. "And you can tell them that for me." He started to turn away, then stopped. "By the way," he said, "who are these people?"

A frightened look came into Harvey's eyes. "Oh, I wouldn't dare to tell you."

"Anyone I know?"

"No! Oh no! They came up from New York. They're part of a big gambling ring."

"Are they the ones who took a shot at me the other night?"

"Took a shot at you?" Harvey feigned surprise. But he didn't fool Dirk.

"Yes, took a shot at me. Or was that you?"

Harvey forced a smile. "Oh, come now; this is no time for humor."

"I am not being humorous. As a matter of fact, I have the bullet which, fortunately, missed me and imbedded itself in that peach tree at the end of the terrace. And if anything more happens up at the house, I may be able to get the police on my side and have them make a search for the gun that shot the bullet. And now if you will excuse me, I have to go up and see my wife."

I said, "I'll wait here," but Dirk took hold of my arm. "No, you'd better come with me," he said, and propelled me along the hall to the elevator, leaving Harvey standing there staring after us with his mouth open and his eyes bulging.

We didn't say anything to each other on the way to Helen's room, but there was no doubt we were both doing a lot of thinking. When we reached Helen's room there was a nurse sitting outside the door. At first she wouldn't let us enter the room, but Doctor Brooks came along and said it was all right. When we opened the door and went into the room, Helen was lying with her eyes closed. There were three other beds in the room, but only one was occupied, by a middle-aged woman who seemed to be asleep.

Dirk went over and kissed Helen, and she opened her eyes. "Oh, Dirk," she murmured, "I'm so glad you've come."

He took her hand and held it in both of his. "I couldn't get away any earlier. We — some people came to the house and — well, anyway, here I am now. How do you feel?"

"Weak and scared."

"There isn't anything to be scared of," Dirk told her with what I knew was more assurance than he felt.

"Yes, there is. I saw somebody shoot at you."

Dirk looked over at the other occupied bed and said, "Ssshhh!"

Helen said, "Oh, she can't hear us. She's under heavy sedation."

Dirk said, "Oh. Well, then tell me, do you remember what happened to you?"

She said, "Yes. It's beginning to come back."

Dirk drew up a chair and sat down close to the bed, and I went and sat in an armchair by a window. Helen smiled at me and said, "Hello, Cheryl."

I said, "Hello, Helen." Then I asked, "Would you like me to wait out in the hall while you talk to Dirk?"

She said, "No. You might as well hear it, in case they catch up with me again."

Dirk smoothed her blonde hair back from her face. "That's what I've been worried about," he said. "I called Doctor Brooks last night and asked him to have you guarded."

She sighed and smiled. "Thank you," she said. "A big husky nurse sat beside my bed all night. This morning I heard someone did try to get into the room in the middle of the night, but the nurse rang for help and I didn't even wake up."

Dirk said, "Good. Now tell me, why did you come up here without letting me know?"

"I was lonesome. So I took Billy up to Mother's and borrowed her car."

"I know that. But where is the car?"

"Oh. Well, I left it on the other side of the green and walked up to the house. I wanted to surprise you. So I walked back toward the terrace. But when I was halfway there, someone grabbed me from behind and dragged me into those bushes at the side." She shuddered and clutched at Dirk's hand. "He put a hand over my mouth so I couldn't scream."

"Could you see who it was?" Dirk asked her.

"No, it was too dark. There were several men, and I heard one of them say, 'Don't hurt her!' His voice was familiar. It could have been Harvey."

"What kept you so long? Your mother said you left there about four."

"I had a couple of flats. And I lost my way a couple of times."

"After a man grabbed you, then what?"

"I saw one of them had a gun, and then you came out of the house and sat down on the terrace, and he pointed the gun at you. But I didn't hear a shot, except when you fired at us. I tried to get away, but the man who was holding me was too strong. And the one who sounded like Harvey must have been hit by your shot, because he grunted and dropped down on the ground. Then something hit me on the back of the head — and that's all I can remember. When I came to it was daylight, but it seemed like a lifetime before John found me and until you and Tony began untying me."

Dirk dropped his face into his hands and groaned. "My God!" he cried. "I might have shot *you!*" Then he took his hands from his face, leaned over and took Helen into his arms and held her tightly for a moment. When he laid her back on the pillow tears were trickling down her white cheeks. "I've been doing a lot of thinking," she said shakily.

Dirk asked, "What about?"

She reached out both hands to him, and he took them. "Us," she said. "I guess I've been kind of mean about your theater projects. I didn't understand how much they meant to you."

Dirk caressed her hands. "Don't worry about it," he said.

"But I do. That is, I will from now on. And when I get out of here I want to stay with you all at the house and — well, help with the picture you're making. I can at least do the house-keeping."

Dirk looked down at their hands for quite a while without speaking. Finally I said, "You'd better tell her about this morning, Dirk. She'll have to know eventually."

She looked at me questioningly. "Know what?"

Dirk answered the question. "Well, we had a little accident over at the house this morning. Vicki fell into the pool and drowned."

Helen gasped. "Oh no!"

Dirk said, "I wasn't going to tell you yet."

Helen sat up, then said, "Ouch!" and leaned back against the pillow, murmuring something about her head. When she could speak again, she said, "How awful! I'll have to get up and go back to the house with you. You'll need your wife there."

Dirk let go of her hands and stood up. "I'll need my wife to get well and strong first of all. And I'm going to see if I can get you moved to a private room and have police protection for you around the clock."

She reached for his hand. "Oh no! I don't want to stay here. I want to go with you."

"Maybe in a couple of days. There's no use your being there at the house while things are in such a muddle."

"But what about the picture?"

"We'll have to forget the picture."

Sincerely Helen said, "Oh, I'm sorry. I truly am."

Dirk leaned over and kissed her. Then he said to me, "You stay here with her until I can make the arrangements for a single room and a policeman to guard it."

I said, "All right."

When Helen and I were alone, with the exception of the sleeping woman in the other bed, I said, "In case you've been thinking you lost your charm bracelet the other night, I have it."

Helen held up her left wrist and looked at it. "That's right," she said. "I haven't got it."

I said, "Tommy found it and brought it in the house to me."

She looked surprised. "Tommy?"

"The cat."

"Oh yes. Didn't Dirk wonder where Tommy found it?"

"Dirk didn't see it. And with all the confusion about the shooting and everything, I thought I'd better not tell him. You see, no one knew you were up here, and then, after somebody had shot at Dirk, Tommy brought in your bracelet. . . ."

She stared at me for a moment. Then the implication began to register and she said, "Oh dear! And you thought maybe I'd shot at Dirk?"

"Well, I didn't know what to think. Anyway, until I was sure I didn't want Dirk to know about the bracelet."

Our eyes met and held, and tears began to run from hers. Then she said, "Thank you. Thank you very much. I know you used to like Dirk and were hurt when he married me. That would have been your chance to get back at me."

"But I don't and never have wanted to get back at you. And since we're on the subject, may I give you a little friendly piece of advice?"

She shrugged. "Why not?"

"Really try to be more understanding of Dirk's love for the theater. It's an incurable disease, and anyone who contracts it never recovers."

She nodded. "I'll do my best. And thank you, Cheryl."

A nurse came into the room, crisp and

breezy. "We're moving you to a better room, Mrs. Halburton," she said. "Just lie still. We'll roll you in, bed and all." The nurse gave her a big smile. "And I'll tell you a little secret. I'm crazy about that big handsome husband of yours."

Helen smiled. "You can't have him," she said. "He's mine."

It didn't take long for them to get Helen settled in a small single room with a nurse on guard until a policeman arrived.

Harvey had gone by the time Dirk and I went downstairs. Doctor Brooks came out of an office along the corridor. "Just a minute," he said. "I'm afraid I have bad news for you."

My heart sank, and Dirk tensed. He asked, "Oh? What?"

"That girl — Vicki something — didn't drown. She was dead before she went into the water."

I grabbed Dirk's arm, and he patted my hand. "But how could that be?" he asked the doctor.

Doctor Brooks looked very serious. "It could be, all right. And it means it wasn't an accident."

I moved closer to Dirk and could feel his body stiffen. He said, "Then someone must have killed her and afterwards thrown her into the water. But who? And how?"

"The pathologist says she was strangled." Doctor Brooks had a stethoscope in his hand,

and he looked down at it as if he were examining it for flaws.

Dirk drew in a heavy breath. "Does that mean the police will be questioning us all again?"

"Quite likely. And then there will have to be an inquest."

Dirk chewed at his upper lip for a moment, then said, "Well, if we have a murderer among us, I suppose the sooner he is discovered the better."

The doctor looked up at him, then said solemnly, "It would seem so."

With a sigh Dirk said, "Well, thanks, Doctor. Please be sure my wife is guarded carefully."

"That will be done."

When we were in my car driving back to the house, I said, "Could one of Harvey's gang have killed Vicki?"

"I suppose it's possible."

I shivered. "I'm beginning to be frightened."

"I wouldn't mind calling in the National Guard myself."

When we got back to the house, Ada had done the dishes and everything was quiet. She was in the living room reading a book. She looked up as we came in. "How's Helen?" she asked.

"Coming along all right," Dirk told her. "Everything all right here?"

"Yes. Charlie is upstairs lying down, and John and Tony are out on the terrace. That man, Joe Hinkley, came by to see if the pool was all right. At least that's what he said. But between you and me, I think he was just nosing around because he'd heard about Vicki."

"Why? Did he ask any questions?"

"Well, he said he'd seen an ambulance and police cars come up here, and he wondered if someone was sick or something."

"What did you tell him?"

"I told him the truth. He'd hear it anyway. I told him Vicki had had an accident and had drowned in the pool."

Dirk sighed and chewed at his upper lip. "What did he say?"

"He said it was too bad, her being such a pretty little girl."

Dirk said, "Um."

"Oh, and he said you'd better keep those mattresses off the floor in the barn, if you ever want to use them again."

Dirk looked surprised. "They are off the floor. They're hanging up over the beams."

I said, "Yes, that's right. I saw them the day we arrived."

Dirk sighed. "I'll go out and take care of them."

He was gone only a few minutes, and when he came back he said, "Damned if two of them weren't on the floor." He sank down in a chair and lit a cigarette. "I suppose I should call Helen's mother."

"And get her car and bring it up here," I suggested.

"That's right. But I haven't the keys."

"They are probably in Helen's purse, wherever that is."

"I don't remember seeing it when we found her."

"Perhaps she dropped it in the bushes when she was attacked."

Without a word Dirk jumped up and strode out of the house, and I after him. We found the purse beneath a bush. It was a white straw clasp-type bag with a thick silk rope handle, and it had evidently been trodden upon by several people. On one side was the dirty imprint of the heel of a man's shoe. I wondered if Sherlock Holmes would have been able to make something out of it.

Dirk picked up the purse and opened it. Everything that would ordinarily be in a woman's purse seemed to be there. Even her wallet and change purse were untouched. And in addition to her own key ring, there was a small leather case with what must have been the keys to her mother's car. The leather case had the name of a Rye automobile salesroom stamped on it in gilt letters. Dirk said, "I'd better go over and bring the car here."

"Want me to drive you?"

He said, "No thanks. I'll walk."

So I went over to the terrace and joined John and Tony. Of course they wanted to know how Helen was, so I told them. I also told them what Harvey had said.

They were both disturbed about this, and John said, "I think we had all better go home. If Dirk wants to stay and fight it out, that's his business, but I don't think the Simmons' or you ought to stay any longer, Cheryl."

"I agree," I said. "We'll never be able to finish the picture with things the way they are. But with this new twist about Vicki, the police may not let us leave."

"What new twist about Vicki?" Tony asked.

"Oh, I forgot to tell you. The autopsy showed she was dead before she went into the water."

"What?" Tony had been reclining in a beach chair with his feet up. Now he sat up straight, and his feet slammed down on the flagstones.

"I'm sorry I had to be the one to tell you, but you have to know. The police are apt to land on us at any minute and start questioning us all over again."

Tony just sat staring at me, but I could tell by the far away look in his eyes that he wasn't seeing me. After a while he said, "The poor kid." Then he looked at John. "But who would — ?"

John shook his head. "I can't imagine," he said. "I know I didn't, and I'm sure you or Dirk wouldn't, and Charlie is too far gone to work up enough energy to kill anybody."

"It could have been one of that gang that wants to buy the house," I suggested.

"Yes, it could," John agreed. "They are apparently a bunch of criminals. But why do they want this particular house? Surely there are other houses they could get."

"Not as many as you might think," I told him. "A couple of years ago my mother thought she'd like to go up farther into the country — she lives in White Plains now. She looked and looked, and you'd be surprised how few houses are available. And this house is unusual. It's located so it isn't noticeable from the main road, and it's large and —" Something in the back of my mind was nudging me. I began to remember what Dirk had said about the house when he had called me and asked me to play the lead in the play. He'd said, "It's an interesting old place. It dates back to the Revolution. One of those 'Washington-Slept-Here' type of places, complete with a getaway tunnel that comes out on the far side of a back field."

"That's it!" I cried, a sudden excitement rising up inside me. "The getaway tunnel!"

"What on earth are you talking about?" Tony asked.

"There is a tunnel somewhere. Dirk told me about it. It comes out on the far side of this back field."

John and Tony exchanged glances and began to smile. John said, "Cheryl darling, I hate to say this, but I think you're cracking up."

"No, I'm not. This is a very old house. It dates back to the Revolution." And I told him what Dirk had told me when he'd phoned me about coming up.

Tony rose. "Come on," he said.

"Where?"

"To the far side of the field, to see if we can find the exit to the tunnel. There is no use looking for the entrance to it in the house. Maybe Dirk knows where it is. Anyway, I'd like to see the exit."

So the three of us almost ran across the field, and at the far side we discovered an old dirt road.

It took us quite a while to find what we were searching for, and then it was only by accident. I tripped over something and, looking to see what, discovered it was a large iron ring set in an iron grating. The whole thing was covered with vines and leaves. I called to the boys, who had gotten ahead of me, and they came back. "Here it is," I told them.

We all peered down through the grating, our heads touching. There wasn't much to see. A flight of crumbling brick steps led down to a depth of about twelve feet, where the tunnel began.

John said, "I don't suppose anyone has a flashlight on him?" Tony and I laughed nervously at the silliness of the idea.

John leaned over and gave a tug at the iron ring, and surprisingly, it lifted the grating easily. Tony grabbed the edge of it, and between them they had it off in no time and laid it on the ground beside the opening.

"Tunnel, anyone?" I asked foolishly.

"You stay here," John ordered. "Tony and I will go down and take a look."

"But I want to go, too."

"No!" John's tone was authoritative. Usually he was easygoing and amenable.

I looked at him in surprise, and he smiled. Then in a pleasanter voice he said, "If there is anything worth seeing, we'll call you."

"All right. But be careful."

The boys went down the stairs cautiously. Several of the steps were wobbly, and it would be easy to turn an ankle.

When they entered the darkness of the tunnel, I had a strange deserted feeling. What if something happened to them down there? Was the tunnel safe structurally? If it dated back to the Revolution, wouldn't it be crumbly, like the steps? And couldn't it cave in and bury them alive?

"Oh no!" I said aloud, and a bird in a tree overhead said, "Chirp!"

I called down the steps, "Are you all right?" But there wasn't any answer. Carefully I began to descend the steps. At the bottom I peered into the tunnel, but it seemed to turn a few yards beyond the entrance, and I couldn't see anything. I called, "Yoohoo! Are you all right?" My voice echoed into the darkness, repeating my words. Then I heard an answering voice but I couldn't understand what it said. Probably, "Don't come in."

But I ventured in as far as the bend, and as I

turned the corner I could see a pinpoint of light — a match flame or a cigarette lighter. I called, "Hello there! Are you all right?" Before my voice had finished echoing, the boys called, "Yes. Go back." Their voices rolled toward me, "Go back! Go back!"

Then something whizzed past my ankles, and I caught my breath. "Rats?"

I hurried back to the turn just in time to see Tommy streaking up the steps. So this was where he'd been? I remembered I hadn't seen him around for a couple of days.

I went back to the turn and carefully on through the darkness until I was near enough to the pinpoint of light to distinguish the faces of the boys. They were examining something stacked up in a niche. "What is it?" I asked.

They turned, and John said, "Go back, Cheryl. We'll be out in a few minutes."

"But what is it?" I persisted.

Tony said, "Money! Bags of it. Some from Chemical Mohegan Bank, some from Manhattan National."

I gasped. "The bank robbers?"

"The same," John said. "Come on; let's get out of here. If they should find us here, we'd be dead ducks."

"But they wouldn't come here in broad daylight!"

John shoved me on ahead of him. "Anybody who would rob two of the biggest banks in the country in broad daylight and get away with it would do anything. Go on, hurry!"

The pinpoint of light went out, and we were in complete darkness. I kept stumbling and banging into the sides of the tunnel. Finally John said, "Let me get ahead of you; then you take my hand." He pushed past me, and we fumbled for each other's hands. I said, "Tony, are you there?"

"Right behind you."

At the turn, a glimmering of daylight made it easier for us, and in a few minutes more we were up the steps and out on the road. The boys lifted the grating into place and covered it again with the vines and leaves. The three of us stood there blinking in the bright sunlight.

We were covered with dust and dirt and began brushing ourselves off.

As we walked across the field, I asked, "What had we better do? Call the police?"

John said, "First we'd better tell Dirk."

He came out of the house as we were nearing the terrace. "Where have you been?" he asked. "I've been looking for you." Then, as we drew closer and he saw our disheveled state, "What happened to you?"

Tony said, "Nothing happened to us, but we've made a dangerous discovery."

"What do you mean?" Dirk's tired face looked haggard.

We all flopped down on chairs before John said, "The tunnel. Cheryl found the exit to it, and we went down."

Dirk sat down and leaned back in a beach chair. "Oh, that," he said. "Harvey and I used to play in it when we were kids."

"Then Harvey knows about it?"

"Oh, sure."

John lit a cigarette. "Well, Harvey plays rougher now."

"What do you mean?"

"You heard about those bank robberies in New York last week?"

"Yes, of course."

"Well, all the money is stacked up in the tunnel. That is, a lot of it is."

"My God!" Dirk jumped to his feet. "Are you sure?"

"Go see for yourself. Only take a good strong flashlight. It's dark in there."

Dirk went into the kitchen and found a flashlight in a drawer. Returning, he said, "Come on. Show me."

John said, "I'll show you. We don't all have to go."

"Wait a minute," I said. "Dirk, do you know where the entrance to the tunnel is? Is it in the house?"

He said, "Yes. There are two: one in the cellar and the other in my room. I'll show you when I get back."

After John and Dirk had started across the field, Tony and I relaxed in the warm sunshine of the terrace. I would have loved a swim, but the memory of Vicki floating there in the pool was too horrifying. I doubted if any of us would go in the pool again.

Tony was stretched out in a beach chair. He closed his eyes, and I guess he dropped off to sleep.

I watched John and Dirk nearing the far side of the field and wondered how the bank robbers dared to leave their cache so unprotected.

But maybe it wasn't as unprotected as it seemed. Surely they must have someone on guard somewhere.

But if there was anyone around, why hadn't he or they stopped us when they saw us going down into the tunnel? Would we have been stopped or shot if we'd brought out any of the loot?

There had been no one on the road, either when we went into the tunnel or when we came out. But it would have been easy for someone to hide behind a bush or a tree and not be seen.

Well, if someone had been and still was around somewhere, then he must surely know the money had been discovered. So now what? Would any of us be safe from now on?

Dirk and John weren't gone long. In just a few minutes I saw them coming back across the field. When they reached the terrace, Dirk said, "I'll call the police right away."

"I wonder if Harvey knows the money is there?" I asked.

Dirk lit a cigarette. His hands were shaking. "I don't know. He may and he may not."

"There is no way to seal off that exit?"

"I can't think of any. We could park a car over the grating. But if they wanted to get in, they would make short work of a car."

"Apparently the money is safer there in the tunnel than it was in the bank." I almost smiled at the ridiculous idea.

Dirk sank into a chair. "If we could incorporate all this into our picture, the TV stations would be fighting for it for a late late show."

"Too bad about the picture," I said. "I think it would have been good, just the way you wrote it."

Dirk managed a smile. "Thanks. My one fan."

"Where are the entrances to the tunnel?" I asked.

"One is in my room, or rather Aunt Suzy's. The bookcase to the right of the fireplace opens, and stairs go down past the cellar entrance. In the cellar there is a certain brick you touch, and part of the wall swings open."

"Then anyone knowing about the tunnel would have access to the house?"

"If they knew the right places to touch."

"Wouldn't Harvey know?"

"Yes. He would know."

"Then that could explain the crying record."

"It easily could." Dirk sat smoking for a minute or so; then he said musingly, "I never liked Harvey, but I had no idea he was such a stinker — or so dangerous."

"If you report the money to the police, won't you implicate Harvey?"

"I don't see how. After all, it is *my* house."

"There will be a lot of newspaper, radio and TV publicity. After all, the money was stolen from two New York City banks."

"Yes, you're right. Maybe I'd better wait for a while before I say anything about it."

"And let the robbers come and get it during the night? And maybe murder all of us?"

"I'd like to get Helen home from the hospital before I say anything."

"But she's under guard."

"I know. But even so, I'd like to be the one guarding her."

So he didn't call the police right away.

Chapter Thirteen

We'd just finished our dinner when the police arrived. Lieutenant Vance came in, and the other man stayed out in the car.

Dirk let the lieutenant in the front door, and Vance asked, "Could I see you all in the living room? I have a few questions."

Dirk said, "Of course." Then to those of us sitting at the dining table, "Come on, all of you." All of us consisted of John, me, Tony, Ada and Charlie, who had come downstairs just in time for dinner, looking very old and sick and not speaking unless he was spoken to.

One by one we got up from our chairs and filed into the living room, seating ourselves in scattered chairs around the room. Lieutenant Vance said, "Suppose we pull the chairs closer together? It will be easier for us to talk." So we regrouped ourselves at the front of the room; Ada and Charlie on a sofa and the rest of us in occasional chairs close by. Lieutenant Vance stood before us, looking down at us like a schoolteacher at a group of pupils. But he didn't seem to be seeing any of us. He wasn't looking at any particular person; he was just standing there as if he were thinking, until we settled down. Then he said, "The reason I wanted to see you is because something disturbing has come to light. Some of you know about it. It's about the little girl who was found in the pool this morning."

We all waited quietly until he began to speak again. "She didn't drown," he said. "She was *murdered* before she went into the water."

Ada gasped and gave Charlie a quick look, but it wasn't quick enough to escape the alert eyes of Lieutenant Vance. "Would you know anything about it?" he asked Charlie, and I suddenly realized no one had told them how Vicki had actually died.

If possible, Charlie's face became grayer than it had been before. There was a haunted look in his eyes, and large drops of perspiration broke out on his forehead and began trickling down his cheeks. "Me? No," he said. "Why should I know anything about it?"

The lieutenant kept looking at him. *"I'm asking you,"* he said.

Charlie shook his head. "I told you all I knew this morning," he said gruffly.

"I don't think you did," the lieutenant persisted.

Ada flounced on her end of the sofa and moved over closer to Charlie so she could put a hand on his arm. "Oh, let him alone!" she cried. "Can't you see he's sick?"

"Is he?" Lieutenant Vance asked. "What's the matter with him?"

She hesitated. "He had a little nervous breakdown and has only been out of the hospital a short time. We came up here so he could have a rest."

"Did you? I thought you came up here to make a picture."

Ada's face flushed. "Well, that too."

The lieutenant looked from one to the other until it was only too evident he was deliberately making both of them very uncomfortable. My heart went out to them. As far as I could see, the lieutenant was wasting his time badgering them. He seemed to think so too, because he turned to Dirk. "How is the picture coming?" he asked.

"Naturally we won't be able to continue with it," Dirk told him.

"Did Mrs. Maretti have an important part in it?" Lieutenant Vance asked.

It was only too apparent he had used Vicki's married name with malice aforethought.

I gave Tony a quick glance and saw his face flush. He drew in his breath, and I thought he was going to say something, but he seemed to change his mind.

Dirk said, "No. Cheryl, Miss Daniels, is the star of the picture."

Lieutenant Vance turned to me. "Then eliminating Mrs. Maretti won't benefit you any?"

I caught my breath. "Of course not!" I said.

He kept looking at me the way he had at Ada and Charlie. "Unless you wanted her husband," he said.

I felt my face flush, and my eyes filled with tears of anger. "That is perfectly stupid!" I cried.

Without taking his eyes from me, he asked, "Tony, is it?"

Tony's mouth tightened at the corners, and a pulse began to throb in his left temple. "It is utterly ridiculous!" he said. "Cheryl and I scarcely know each other except professionally. Besides, my wife and I have been divorced for five years. So if Cheryl wanted me — or I wanted her — there was nothing standing in our way."

"Except me," John said quietly.

"Why you?" Lieutenant Vance asked him.

"Because Cheryl and I were engaged."

My heart gave a jump, and my eyes flew to John's face.

"I thought you and Miss Daniels broke your engagement two years ago."

John smiled. "So you've been doing your homework."

"It's my business to do my homework," the lieutenant told him somewhat crossly.

"I'm sorry," John said, "but I'm afraid we're a little ahead of you. We've renewed our engagement. Or perhaps the word is reestablished it. Haven't we, Cheryl?"

What could I do but back him up? A bit shakily I said, "That's right." Then, to make it sound more authentic, I added, "Mrs. Harvey Halburton knows that. We told her a couple of days ago."

The lieutenant walked over to the fireplace and stood looking down into it for several moments, with his back to us. Then he whirled around. "How many of you were down by the pool this morning before Miss Daniels discovered the body of Mrs. Maretti floating in it?"

No one spoke. Finally Dirk said, "Nobody was. We were all in bed, asleep."

The lieutenant looked around at each of us in turn. "Somebody was," he said.

"Oh, you're just guessing," Ada said disparagingly.

He glanced over at her. "Am I?" he asked. "Or did you just overlook the puddle of water beside your husband's bed this morning?"

She gasped, then lowered her face into her hands and began to cry silently.

Charlie jumped up. He seemed to have aged twenty years. "All right! So I did it! I threw her into the pool! I went down to the terrace early this morning to get some air because I couldn't sleep, and she was asleep there on the terrace on one of the beach chairs. She didn't have anything on but one of those short mini things, and she was so beautiful I went kind of crazy and tried to make love to her. But she was dead. At first I thought she was pretending to be asleep; then I realized she felt cold and strange. And I couldn't wake her up. Then I realized she was dead. And I didn't know what to do. I was afraid everybody would think I killed her. And I didn't. I got scared, so I picked her up and carried her over to the pool and dropped her into the water. And the water splashed all over me!"

"Then what?" Lieutenant Vance asked quietly.

"Then I went upstairs and told Ada, my wife. And she made me get into bed. And we just waited."

"For what?" the lieutenant asked.

"For someone to discover the body."

Ada jumped up and threw her arms around him and sobbed against his shoulder. He just held her close, his cheek resting against her hair.

Tears of pity for them both began rolling down my cheeks, and Tony, John and Dirk sat perfectly still, as if they'd been turned to stone.

It seemed an eternity before anyone spoke, and then I was surprised to hear my own voice saying, "Then we still don't know who actually murdered Vicki."

Slowly Lieutenant Vance turned to me. "You are right, Miss Daniels," he said. "But until we do, I am afraid I shall have to arrest Mr. Simmons — or at least take him into protective custody."

Dirk jumped up. "Why can't he just be left here, in *my* custody?" he asked.

Lieutenant Vance shook his head. "I'm afraid not, Dirk. There have been too many strange things going on here. Frankly, I don't think any of you are safe here."

Ada raised her head. Her face was blotchy, her eyes colorless from weeping. "Please!" she pleaded. "Don't take my husband away. He's no murderer; just a foolish old man." And she began to cry again.

The lieutenant went over and pried her arms loose from Charlie's neck. "I'm sorry," he said. "But there has been one murder here, and we don't want any more."

Chapter Fourteen

After Lieutenant Vance had left with the defeated, dejected and frightened Charlie, and the rest of us had spent quite a while getting Ada quieted down, Dirk said, "Just so we have something to do, why don't we shoot the beginning of that first scene of the second act — the part where Deborah and Allister get out of bed and Allister goes into the bathroom and then Deborah calls her father on the phone? We can shoot it up to where Rosemary is supposed to come in. What do you say, Tony?"

Tony shrugged. "All right with me. The light won't be right. It was supposed to be morning. But I guess I can fake it. I'll take up the lights and the camera and tape recorder."

Dirk said, "I'll go up and arrange the furniture. John and Cheryl, get your scripts."

I said, "Mine is up in my room." John said, "Mine is upstairs, too." So we went up the stairs together. When we reached the second floor, John put a hand on my arm. "Did you mind me telling the lieutenant we were engaged?"

I turned and looked up at him, and a strange thing happened. I suddenly realized I didn't love him any more. For two long years I had

178

thought I was brokenhearted because our engagement had come to an end. And then when we met in Mount Sharon, I began to feel his attraction working on me again. And when he'd kissed me in the dining room that first morning, my old feeling for him had flared up again, more intense than before. Now, for no particular reason, he didn't stir me at all. The realization was frightening. What had happened to me? Had the tragedies of the last few days numbed me?

Before I could answer John's question, Tony started up the stairs, carrying the camera tripod over one broad shoulder. The hall light shone down on his soft black hair, and his clean-cut profile was silhouetted against the scenic paper on the wall of the hall stairway. My heart fluttered, quickened its beat, and a feeling of exultation rose within my breast. "Oh no!" I cried aloud. My meaning was perfectly clear to me, but John thought I was answering his question and said, "That's good. Because I mean it."

Before I could say anything more, Tony had arrived at the top of the stairs and stopped beside us. "Go get your nightie on," he told me, "and get into bed." Then he called to Dirk, "Hey, Dirk, help me with the rest of the lights, will you?"

Dirk came out of his room into the hall. "Sure," he said. "Everything is okay in the bedroom."

John said, "I'll change to my pajamas and be right there," and went along to the room he shared with Tony.

As I changed to my nightie, I wondered if I should have realized what was happening to me and recognized my growing feeling for Tony when I was the only one who was upset because he had disappeared yesterday and not returned by dinner time. No one else had been particularly upset about it.

I put my robe over my nightie, put on my bedroom slippers and went into Dirk's room, also taking the things I was supposed to put on later in the scene. While the boys were getting the lights and camera set up and the tape recorder placed, I planted my clothing in bureau drawers. Then I wandered over to the fireplace and began feeling around for the secret panel that opened onto the stairs to the tunnel. I felt on all the bookshelves, moved books and peered behind them, but found nothing.

Dirk came in with a light and grinned at me. "You'd never find it on your own," he told me. He put the light down, came over and reached a hand up inside the fireplace. Slowly the bookcase on the right began to open onto a dark passage that disclosed a steep, narrow flight of stairs going down into unknown depths.

I peeked in, then backed up. "It's spooky," I said.

Dirk laughed, reached his hand inside the fireplace again, and the bookcase began to close.

John and Tony came over. "That the entrance to the tunnel?" John asked.

Dirk said, "Yes. Want to see?"

John came over to the bookcase. "Sure," he said.

Tony finished with a light and joined us, stuck his head inside, then backed away. "Something tells me you should have told the police about that money," he said.

Dirk said, "I'd sort of like to have a talk with Harvey first."

"And let him warn the robbers that you know the money is there?" I asked. "You know you're life wouldn't be worth a plugged nickel if they ever learned you or any of us had discovered their hiding place."

Tony said, "No. And I think you should consider the girls. Their lives aren't safe, either, with the setup as it is. Look what happened to Helen and Vicki."

Dirk sighed. "I realize that. And I'm as worried as you are. But — oh, well, let's shoot this scene. Then we'll go down to the kitchen and have some coffee and talk about it."

Tony set up his lights the way he wanted them, put the camera on the tripod and said, "Okay, Cheryl, you and John get into bed."

Ada came from her room and stood in the doorway. "May I watch?" she asked. I knew she'd been having a good cry all alone in her room. And who could blame her? She'd tried to cover her blotched face with makeup, but the

181

redness of her eyes was still only too evident.

Dirk said, "Sure. Come on in. But stay out of the line of the camera."

"How about me sitting over there in the rocking chair?"

Quickly Dirk said, "No. Take that other chair."

Tony had everything ready, and John and I got into bed. Tony panned in on the scene as Allister and Deborah were getting *out* of bed. We went through the scene to the place where Allister goes into the bathroom and starts the shower. Then I, as Deborah, go to the phone to call my father — the part Charlie had been taking, of course keeping a finger on the button so I wouldn't flash the operator. When Dirk mimicked Charlie's voice coming over the phone, Ada caught her breath; but realizing the tape recorder was turned on, she managed not to make an audible sound.

I, as Deborah, was in the middle of the conversation with my father on the phone, sitting on the side of the bed, when I saw the bookcase at the right of the fireplace begin to open slowly. Tony, operating the camera, had panned in on a close-up of me, but out of the corner of my eye I could see him slowly moving back with the camera to get the entire room. Dirk was standing to one side with a script in his hand and had his back to the fireplace.

I held my breath as I saw a stocky masked man come out of the opening to the tunnel. He had a gun in his hand. "Don't anybody move or

I'll shoot," he said in a gravelly-sounding voice.

None of us did. Then he began to walk over to me, at the same time keeping a wary eye on Dirk and Ada. John was still in the bathroom, and Ada was too frightened to move. I doubt if the man even noticed Tony. If he had he would have surely shot at him and the camera.

"You!" he said to me. "Get into the tunnel."

I just stared at him, frozen into immobility with fear, but still with enough presence of mind to release the little button on the phone, hoping against hope that a telephone operator might hear what was going on.

Dirk whirled around and began to make a move toward the man, but the intruder was too quick for him. Instantly the gun was pointing at Dirk's heart. "Stay where you are!" he commanded. "I'll deal with you later. But first I'll take the girl."

He reached out a hand and grabbed my shoulder, and I screamed.

Then everything happened at once. The empty rocking chair suddenly began to rock, faster and faster. Then it flew up into the air, sailed across the room and hit the masked man in the head. Surprised, he cried out, and the gun dropped from his hand as he and the rocking chair crashed to the floor together. Then Ada screamed, and John rushed out of the bathroom in his robe, asking, "What's the matter? I heard something on the phone in the john." When he saw the masked man on the floor with the rocking chair turned upside down on top of him, he motioned to Dirk, and the two of them leaped at the man simultaneously. Then Tony, who up to that moment had kept working the camera, left it and rushed to me, pulling me up into his arms. Holding me tight, he said, "It's all right now. No one is going to hurt you. I wanted to get a picture of him, but I'd never have let him take you."

The feeling of his strong arms about me and the hardness of his body against mine were all I needed to feel safe and protected. But my feeling of security was short-lived.

The next thing I knew, Harvey was coming into the room from the opened bookcase, and Joe Hinkley appeared at the hall doorway. Harvey didn't have a gun but Joe did. Harvey's arm was still in a sling. In a moment I saw he was being prodded in the back by a gun held by another masked man. This one was of medium height and thin, but he had a menacing manner, and there was no doubt that he meant business. He said, "Let my friend alone!" With his gun pointed at them, Dirk and John had no choice but to release the man they were holding.

Dirk cried, "Harvey! What is the meaning of this?"

Harvey, as white as the proverbial sheet, looked frightened and was shaking. "Sorry about this, Dirk," he said. "But the whole thing is out of my hands."

The man behind him growled, "Shut up and you won't get hurt. We want the guy who owns the house!"

"I own the house," Dirk said. "What do you want?"

The first man, who had managed to wrench free of Dirk and John, get out from beneath the rocking chair and retrieve his gun, said, "The house. We want the house."

Dirk said, "You won't get it."

Both masked men started toward Dirk, guns pointed at him, but Dirk stood his ground. "Killing me won't get you the house," he told them.

"Oh, yes, it will," the thin man said, pulling a piece of paper out of his pocket. "Because before we kill you, you're going to sign the house over to us."

"No I'm not!" Dirk said. If he was frightened, he wasn't showing it.

Then Tony let go of me, made a sign to John, and he and John jumped the two men. It was a trick I'd seen done in *Stars Away,* and it was beautiful. Harvey just stood there. Ada and I cried, "Be careful," just as the sound of a shot blasted through the room. The first masked man dropped to the floor again, this time with blood running down his shirt front. The second man began to struggle with Tony and John, but Tony had knocked his gun to the floor. I rushed and grabbed it, sticking it into the man's back.

At first I hadn't been sure from which gun the shot had been fired. Then I saw it was Joe

Hinkley's gun that was smoking. I said, "Good shot, Joe," but he turned away and ran down the stairs.

Tony and John had quite a tussle to subdue the man they were holding, and I had to back away because I didn't want to shoot him unless I had to. Fortunately, I didn't have to, because simultaneously a policeman appeared in the door to the hall and from behind the opened bookcase. They both had guns cocked and went over and took the man into custody. Then several more policemen came out of the opening to the tunnel, and in no time at all the place was in pandemonium. Even Emma Halburton and Annie from the restaurant arrived, probably having seen all the police cars scooting up the road. But the police quickly shoved them away and told them to go home.

After it was all over, we learned that the police had traced the bank robbers up to Mount Sharon, and when strange things began to happen on Dirk's property they began to keep a watch.

Under questioning, Joe Hinkley said he'd been keeping an eye out because of the mattresses on the floor of the barn. He knew Mr. Dirk wouldn't have put them there. So he just happened to see the two masked men get Harvey and drag him into the tunnel. Joe had run and phoned the police, then had gotten his gun and come up through the house to help Harvey if he could. After more questioning, he admitted to having killed Vicki — quite by accident. He had come over early that morning to do some gardening before it got too hot, and there Vicki was asleep on a beach chair in her mini-nightdress. It had been too much of a temptation to Joe, whose wife was fat and unattractive and no longer amorous. So he had started to make love to Vicki while she was asleep. But she had awakened, started to fight him and tried to scream. So he had had to silence her. He was sorry, because she was such a pretty little girl. Then he had run away, leaving her dead there on the beach chair, where Charlie had found her a little later.

The bank robber Joe Hinkley had shot died, and the other confessed, naming other confederates, but absolving Harvey of any part in the bank robberies. However, Harvey confessed he'd planted the crying record and had tried to frighten his aunt into leaving the house and going into a nursing home. "That," said Dirk, "was probably the reason she kept a gun in her knitting basket."

"Did she?" Harvey asked. "Why, the crazy old fool!"

Chapter Fifteen

And that ended Dirk's attempt to film his own movie. But he no longer cared. The most important thing was that Helen was safe. As soon as everything was over, he took her home to their New York apartment. And now she is working with him on a new story to be filmed in their apartment and around the city.

John began rehearsing next season's *Stars Away* series, and Tony got a good part in an off Broadway show and was a guest performer on several TV shows. I went back to making TV commercials and was only too glad to do it. Some day I would get out of the rut, but after my experience in Mount Sharon I was glad just to be safe.

The experience, bad as it was, helped Charlie to pull himself together, and he is going to be in a new musical comedy in the fall.

John and I are drifting apart again, but I've been seeing a lot of Tony. He is a dear, and he seems to enjoy my company. As a matter of fact, the other evening he said, "You know, Cheryl, you're showing me what real love is. I'd decided there was no such thing, and for five years I kept girls out of my life. But our time up there at Mount Sharon showed me what a real nice girl was like, and I'm beginning to want to get married again, this time for keeps." Then he drew me into his arms and kissed me, and I knew that it would be for keeps, for both of us.

Oh, yes, I almost forgot one thing. When Dirk got the rushes of as much of the picture as was on film, he had us all over to the apartment for a showing. It was too bad we weren't able to do the entire picture, because what we had done was really good, even the part that wasn't supposed to be, where the masked man came in and the rocking chair flew across the room and hit him in the head. In that part there was a misty figure in the rocking chair. It looked like an elderly woman in a long negligee. And believe it or not, she began rocking the chair furiously; then she got up, picked up the chair and threw it so it sailed through the air and hit the masked man in the head.

We all cried out, and I asked, "Dirk, what was that? Who? Did you see that? Run that part again!"

He did, and the misty figure was unmistakably in the picture, in living color. It wasn't just a trick of lighting or a figment of someone's imagination.

Tony said, "Strange. I couldn't see her when I was working the camera."

Dirk smiled. "Well, she was there," he said. "Blessed old Aunt Suzy."

We hope you have enjoyed this Large Print book. Other Thorndike Press or Chivers Press Large Print books are available at your library or directly from the publishers.

For more information about current and up-coming titles, please call or write, without obligation, to:

Thorndike Press
P.O. Box 159
Thorndike, Maine 04986 USA
Tel. (800) 223-1244
Tel. (800) 223-6121

OR

Chivers Press Limited
Windsor Bridge Road
Bath BA2 3AX
England
Tel. (0225) 335336

All our Large Print titles are designed for easy reading, and all our books are made to last.